Dr. Galen's Little Black Bag

Dr. Galen's Little Black Bag

STORIES

R. A. Comunale, M.D.

Mountain Lake Press
Mountain Lake Park, Maryland

ALSO BY R.A. COMUNALE

Requiem for the Bone Man
Berto's World
The Legend of Safehaven

LIBRARY OF CONGRESS
CONTROL NUMBER: 2009925950

ISBN: 978-0-9814773-5-0

ISBN-10: 0-9814773-5-6

PRINTED IN THE UNITED STATES OF AMERICA

MOUNTAIN LAKE PRESS
24 D STREET
MOUNTAIN LAKE PARK, MD 21550

FIRST EDITION, SEPTEMBER 2009

BOOK AND COVER DESIGN BY MICHAEL HENTGES

CONTENTS

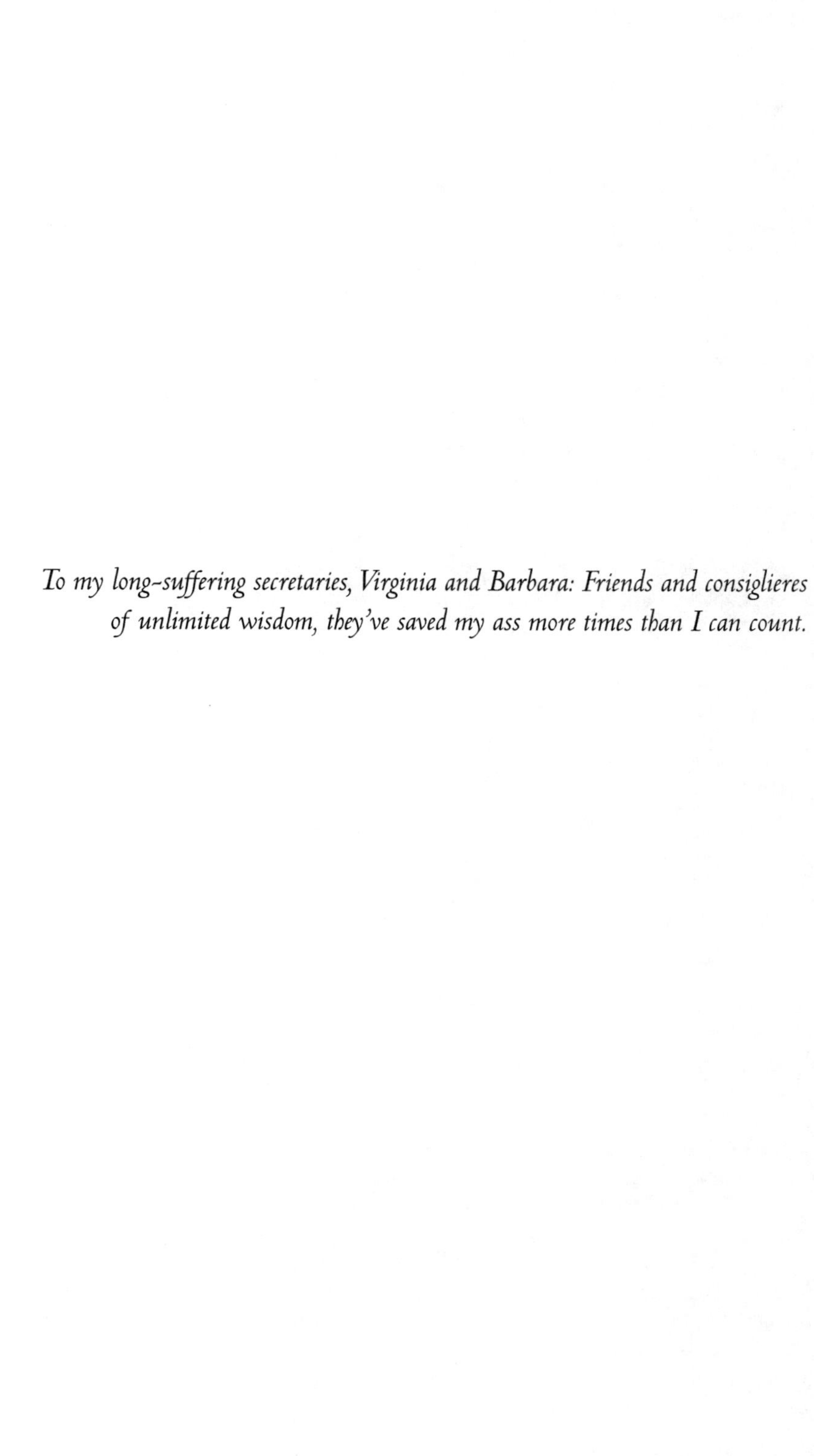

To my long-suffering secretaries, Virginia and Barbara: Friends and consiglieres of unlimited wisdom, they've saved my ass more times than I can count.

PROLOGUE

Hey, Mistah, wanna buy a duck?
He don' need no duck, kid. He's a quack.
Hey, Rube!

I know that I'm old ... over four score ... but I'm not senile.

Just because I fall asleep in my chair, mouth open and snoring to beat the band, I still have all my faculties ... I think.

So why the hell am I hearing voices?

I'm up here, Gazoonie!

It sits on my shelf, companion to the stuffed toy dog my beloved Leni brought me that last day of her life.

A black-leather doctor's bag.

It sits there, mute testimony to over sixty years of interacting with the lives of countless patients.

Did I say mute?

Yeah, Galen, it's me. You haven't held me in a coon's age, have you?

Like me it's well-worn, the gold lettering on its side now faded and illegible; its surface scuffed and cracked.

Well, ain't you curious, old man?

I rise from my chair. I reach up, take hold of the handles, sit back down, and set it on my lap.

I open it. Its hinges creak stiffly, just like mine.

Inside I see my old friends: bottles, glass ampoules, and rubber-stoppered vials with faded labels; worn, metal gadgets that would make today's doctors laugh at the primitive state of medicine once practiced. I do not remind them that such shamanism kept their parents, grandparents, and great-grandparents alive to carry on their genetic whirlpool.

Now ya got it, old man. Remember?

Yes, I do. There's the old scalpel I used in cadaver lab. Don't know why I kept it. Never used it on anyone living . . . I think.

Hey, Galen, you really did a hatchet job on me, didn't you? You got damned big fingers to go poking around my insides.

Harry? You here, too?

Patients who endured the fumbling of a medical student and survived; patients who became my friends and extended family; young patients who stroked my ego by following in my footsteps—all peering up at me from that bag.

Doc, look what ya made us do! Ya sure ya ain't the devil?

Listen, guys, can I help it if you were foolish enough to become doctors? Crescenzi, Criswell, Shepland, all of you—admit it. You wanted it, too, didn't you?

Yeah, and you were just some innocent recruiter, weren't you? Come on, Doc, you conned us into it. We never got our seventy-two virgins, either!

Heh, heh, so I lied, guys. Sue me!

I see other things as well: my passions, my loves, my failures, and . . . my few successes? I see the rich, the poor, the famous, and the unknown. In the end all shared the same human traits: the boy who shot himself in order to live; the child with Down's syndrome, who understood more than most; the politicians whose idiosyncrasies would startle and disgust their followers, and the quiet lives of heroes and cowards.

I return it to my shelf, not-so-mute testimony to sixty years of my life.

My little black bag. The one life companion the Bone Man could not take from me.

—Robert Anthony Galen, M.D. (retired)

When Harry Met Sal

Hey, Berto, let me outta this damned thing!

Sal, is that you?

Sho'nuff, Dottore.

What the hell am I doing here, Sal?

Don't you know, kid?

"Wake up, City Boy! No bad dreams today."

My roommate, Dave, stood over me wearing only his birthday suit.

"Wha . . . what's going on?"

I lay in a cold sweat, almost as naked as Dave, sprawled half in, half out of my dorm bed.

"You were yellin' at somebody named Sal."

I shook my head. I couldn't get the image out of my mind: my dead friend Salvatore zipped up in a rubber body bag.

"Come on, roomie, let's hit the showers. Can't keep the dean waitin'!"

"Welcome, sons and daughters of Aesclepius!"

My mind's eye sees them all: the extroverted, the silent, the hand shakers and the wallflowers. I remember the ones who made it through four years of medical boot camp and the ones who did not.

It was the first day—young men and women vibrating with an awareness of something indescribable—that magical first day of medical school, that first day of the rest of our lives.

Today's young doctors tell me their initiation as acolytes of the son of Apollo began with a white-coat ceremony: Friends and family watch, while dignitaries bestow the traditional garb on each new student. Each dons it as a vestment of the priesthood he or she is about to enter, while the Oath of Hippocrates is recited by candlelight.

Youngsters! We had no such elegance. Neither did we share in a very wonderful and new tradition of honoring the memory of those who had bequeathed their bodies, so we could learn from the mortality of others.

No, we had the black bag.

We listened with half-baked attention, while the dean and other school officials welcomed us, but our eyes kept darting toward a row of tables at the side of the conference room.

There sat more than a hundred small, black-leather bags—real doctors' bags—enticing and bewitching us with their silent siren call. Not fancy and not big. Those would come later; these were easily recognizable as student bags.

And yet—and yet—they held the tools of our future trade: a simple stethoscope, a little metal hammer with a triangular rubber head that made us giddy, as we laughed and tapped one another's knees to watch the involuntary-reflex twitching, and more.

We had to buy the sphygmomanometers—aka blood-pressure cuffs—and the fancy flashlights called oto-ophthalmoscopes. We bruised our arms trying them out. We also nearly blinded ourselves by shining the white-and-green lights in our eyes, and we induced bleeding in our auditory canals, when we jammed the dark-green, plastic speculums into fellow students' ears.

Do not laugh.

We clutched those bags tightly, as we walked back to our dormitories, ignoring the knowing smiles and outright derision of the upper classmen. We didn't care.

"Ow! Damn it, Dave, go easy with the cuff!"

Dave assumed that maximum inflation was necessary in his first attempts to take my blood pressure. My arm was frequently numb and swollen.

"You're burnin' a hole in my retina, you moron!"

Ah, yes, the moron was me. My initial ineptitude at trying to visualize the back of the eye—the retina and the optic disc—gave him many a migraine.

Dave, whom I called Country Boy, and I served as guinea pigs for one another. We'd hold open our *Textbook of Physical Diagnosis* and listen and thump and blind each other in desperate attempts to imitate the "correct way" of examining patients. It didn't matter that we still knew squat about the human body. It also didn't matter that we were embarrassed to hell and back at the more intimate examinations, which were more painful than a baseball to the groin. We were playing doctor, and this time it was for real.

"Oh, God, today's gross anatomy lab."

My classmate Carol's tiny voice quivered, as we trotted across the campus to that first lab session. Back then the anatomy lab was held in a different building—a dirty, red-brick, Civil War relic without air conditioning—and we arrived at the door out of breath.

"Hey, City Boy, what the hell are those things on the walls?"

I had to laugh. Dave was a weed-thin, Lynchburg farm boy. If he had grown up in my tenement neighborhood back in Newark, and had gone to my ancient elementary school run by nuns, he would easily have recognized gaslight fixtures that predated the electric light.

A bald-headed gnome and a parrot-faced woman waited impatiently, until we settled down.

The gnome harrumphed.

"Ladies and gentlemen, I'm John Hedley. This is Mrs. Gertrude Gable, my assistant. There are some rules of behavior that we expect—no, demand—of you."

Gable's gravelly voice cut in.

"You will be assigned four to a table. You will wear your lab smocks and gloves at all times. I hope you are wearing shoes and clothes that you won't miss at the end of the year. You won't want to keep them."

Dave and I looked quizzically at each other.

"What the hell is she talkin' about?" he mouthed.

But Gravel Gertie was right; I still have my shoes. Sixty years later I can still smell the formaldehyde. It never did come out. The clothes and green smock are long gone, more the product of diet than a lack of sentimentality. I'm still good looking but not as svelte as I used to be.

"At no time will you be disrespectful of the bodies you will be working on. Treat them as you would want your own body to be treated."

Hear that, kid? Did those police docs treat mine with respect?

Sal, you're dead. You don't belong here!

Can you think of a better place for a dead guy to be, Berto?

I noticed Hedley staring at my name tag.

"Mr. Galen, did you have something to say?"

"Uh ... no, sir. Sorry, sir."

Hedley cast a baleful glance at me then held up a pudgy hand and wagged a finger at us.

"If I catch anyone being an ass, violating these bodies in any way, I will have you expelled right then and there. Do you understand?"

Was he looking right at me?

We nodded. Why would anyone even think of doing something as grotesque as violating a cadaver?

You are one dumb shit, Berto.

Get outta my head, Sal.

Unh-uh, kiddo. Just wait. You'll be glad I'm here.

I was no stranger to death. My old neighborhood hosted a charter chapter of the unexpected-death club. I met my first member when I was eight years old—my beautiful Marigold Lady of the river, a casualty of a back-alley abortion. Still, I admit, nearly six decades later, I felt a cold chill, as Hedley took a key from his vest pocket and unlocked the lab door.

The odor. That's what hits you first. The vapors of the preservative liquids assault your nose and forever imprint themselves on your olfactory lobes in that most primitive part of your brain. You never forget it.

So, there we stood, dressed in green lab smocks and staring at row upon row of stainless-steel tables. On each lay a dark-brown, rubber bag, its contents elevating the fabric in the unmistakable shape of a human body. It was a classroom of the dead.

"Pair off in fours."

Two on each side, we all stared down at those zippered containers then jumped as Gable rasped, "Open your bags!"

The four of us eyed one another, each waiting for someone else to make the first move. We were two guys and two girls: Dave and me, Carol and Tara. The females glanced at us males with nervous smiles, and we tried to feign nonchalance.

But no one touched that zipper.

"Come on, come on!" Hedley's voice was almost Mel Blanc in quality.

You heard Porky Pig, Dottore Berto, go for it!

As the great Yogi Berra once said, it was déjà vu all over again.

For a moment I was back home, standing in the police morgue beside my mentor, Dr. Corrado Agnelli. Salvatore Gatto—my best and only surviving, early boyhood friend Sal—had been brought there. My clothes were still covered with blood and bone spatters from the shotgun blasts that had taken his life an hour before.

Now Sal's mutilated body lay on the same, stainless-steel table that had cradled my Marigold Lady thirteen years earlier.

"Corrado, I can't go through with this. I can't!"

The dead lady had decided my life's work; Sal's death had made me question my resolve.

"You must, Berto, for Sal's sake … and your own."

I watched the police surgeons dissect what had once been a friend, the person who had been my surrogate brother.

You heard Agnelli, Berto. Show me ya got the balls ta do it.

Shut up, Sal!

Chicken!

Cut it out, for cryin' out loud!

Chicken shit, chicken shit!

I took a breath. My hand moved forward and grasped the zipper. I felt my classmates' hands rest on my own. Together we pulled it down.

Bravo, Dottore, bravo!

Grazie, Sal.

"City Boy, you okay?"

Dave was shaking me.

I opened my eyes.

"Huh? Oh … uh … yeah, Dave. Sorry guys."

The girls smiled at me. It made me feel good.

Now, wasn't that worth it, paisan?

Suddenly we heard retching and a male voice crying out, "Oh, sweet Jesus!" and then the sound of a collapsing body.

Hedley and Gable raced to that table and helped our classmate stand back up.

"He worked for my father! He used to play with me when I was a kid!"

Chet's tearful voice kept repeating those words. Hedley and Gable re-zipped the bag and wheeled the cart out of the lab. Within minutes the morgue attendant had arrived with another body.

We began examining our cadaver.

In life he had been a big man, powerfully built, like a boxer. African-American, he didn't appear to be older than his mid-to-late forties. What could have killed a man like this? We would soon find out.

Hey, Sal, bet this is what you'd have looked like in twenty-five years!

No answer.

"Listen up, peepuwl."

Jeez, now he's Elmer Fudd!

Hedley continued: "What happened to your colleague this morning is a reminder; death overtakes us all. At some point, each and every one of you will see someone close to you—someone you know—die."

Carol nodded.

I remembered Angie, Tomas, and especially Salvatore; all my early childhood friends now gone, snatched from life before my very eyes.

"We're going to remove the brain first. It's the most fragile and difficult organ to preserve and some may ... uh ... not be in ... uh ... good shape."

Gable and Hedley exchanged glances.

At that remark a group of graduate anatomy students arrived, each carrying an electric, circular saw and a large, morgue scalpel. One walked to our table and, as we watched, he made a semicircular cut two-thirds around the cadaver's scalp. He reached out and in one, sock-removing motion, pulled the scalp up and forward. Then he placed the saw against the now-bare skull, and the rotating blade easily cut through the bone.

Dead bone smells like burning dog hair when it's cut.

"*Voila!* Ladies and gentlemen, I give you the human brain."

Our graduate student bowed, as we applauded.

Once more the sounds of retching, but this time it was a response to the terrible, rotting-flesh odor filling the air.

"Sorry, folks," Hedley said, "but as I told you, sometimes the preservative doesn't reach the brain."

Damned good thing my brain was fresh, right Berto?

Sal, you didn't have one.

That wasn't an insult. One of the shotgun blasts had taken half of Sal's head off.

Two rows down a foul-smelling pablum oozed from the brain case of the cadaver lying there.

The graduate student at the table cleaned up the mess. Meanwhile Hedley and Gable circulated, eventually reaching us.

"Ah, splendid!" Hedley gushed, as he noted our cadaver's intact brain.

Well, not truly intact. A large, preserved blood clot had indented a good portion of the left side.

"This is wonderful, students. It's obvious what killed this man."

Gable seemed in ecstasy.

Whatever turns ya on, lady.

Shut up, Sal.

Our cadaver, whom we soon nicknamed "Harry," had died of a massive stroke. A major artery had ruptured in his brain, probably killing him instantly. In life, like many African-Americans, he had suffered from uncontrolled high blood pressure. Unfortunately, like most men of any skin color back then, he probably ignored the symptoms or had no inkling that he had a problem.

I think of the myriad drugs we have today to treat elevated blood pressure, and the ethnic-specific drugs that can be even more effective. Back then we had fluid pills—diuretics—and a drug called alpha methyl dopa, which caused people to pass out when they stood up too quickly. Our biggest gun was a hideously powerful and unstable medication called nitroprusside. It often killed more than it helped.

Once more Hedley's voice changed, this time a close match to Daffy Duck.

Wonder if he can do Bugs Bunny.

"Each of you has your disthecting kit, yeth?"

His pronunciation of "dissecting" would have made Daffy or even Sylvester the Cat proud.

We all nodded. The wallet-sized, plastic kit held a large, bladed scalpel, semi-dull scissors, pointed probe, and tweezers.

"For the most part, the best tools you have will be your fingers," Gable added.

Quit lickin' yer chops, Berto.

I couldn't help it; I let out a snorting laugh, which drew a glare from Gravel Gertie.

Later we found out that her hoarse voice was the result of a rare condition affecting her vocal cords. It would ultimately take her life.

"Blunt dissection is always your best bet. You won't damage structures that way."

While we looked on, Hedley's hands reached like ice-cream scoops on either side of Harry's brain, his gloved fingers gently loosening the tissues from the boney case we call the skull. He motioned for me to cut underneath where the telephone cables of the brain—what ultimately becomes the spinal cord—exit through the base of the skull.

The entire class watched Hedley triumphantly holding that tan-gray object above his head like a proud father.

All that Harry had once been, all that he had once felt and experienced—love, hate, happiness, despair, ecstasy—vibrated as electrical and chemical impulses through that amazingly compact, organic computer.

Where was Harry now?

Ya don' wanna know, kid.

Days, weeks, months passed. Gradually we got to know Harry more intimately than any partner he had had in life. We spent extra time on weekends and evenings studying him, often bringing snacks and sandwiches to munch on. We'd quiz one another on the various structures such as Harry's cigarette-smoke-stained lungs, his enlarged heart surrounded by fat, his coronary arteries already almost completely occluded. If the stroke hadn't killed him Harry would have died almost as quickly from a massive heart attack. And if that hadn't done him in, the aneurysm in his aorta, a balloon-like weakness in the artery wall, would have sparked a fatal hemorrhage, if someone had punched him in the gut—or even if he had sneezed too hard.

Harry's other internal organs were no better. His liver was also enlarged, and his pancreas was scarred from too much alcohol. His gallbladder was filled with stones, his kidneys shrunken, the effect of the prolonged, high blood pressure.

This man had felt pain and ignored it for most of his adult life.

No doubt about it, Harry had lived hard and died young. The scarring from gonorrhea and syphilis, and the premature enlargement of his prostate, betrayed his penchant for the ladies.

The only organs that seemed intact were his stomach and intestines—until Gable pointed out the ulcers, a result of his alcohol intake.

We examined Harry's muscles, separating each one out and noting how it created a particular motion. It was a difficult study; the preservative fluids had made the muscle fibers brittle, and the evaporation and drying out made them less comprehensible.

We spent time on another cadaver as well—a necessity for learning the distaff anatomy. During our first trade, we learned that the other group had named her "Shirley."

Reminds me of the gal that was with me when I got whacked. Remember her, Berto?

The old nursery rhyme is wrong; women aren't made of sugar and spice, and not everything is nice. They, too, can live hard lives and suffer the consequences, often more severely than their male counterparts.

Sometimes I dream of Harry and Shirley.

Did they ever meet in life?

By early spring we had reduced our cadaver to many pieces. We had been tested many times on him and the other bodies in grimoire-march practical exams.

We had suffered routines like this throughout college, moving in single file past various stations of the biologic cross, given twenty seconds to identify ambiguous structures in sea creatures, plants, frogs, cats, and dogs.

Now the human counterpart challenged us: dried-out pieces of humanity with pins stuck through them and a question scribbled alongside that taxed our brains.

One: What the hell was that small, dried-out, macaroni-like tube that bore no resemblance to its real-life appearance?

Two: What did it do?

Three: What other action did it work against?

And so on.

Our first year was coming to an end. We had studied the normal aspects of the human body: its chemistries, its physiology, and its large, small, and microscopic structures. We had attended physical-diagnosis sessions, seeing and talking to live patients. At first clumsy and uncertain, then with more and more self-assurance, we examined them in front of our professors.

Each time we attended, we carried our little black bags like talismans, self-consciously removing the tools of our trade, as we performed for grades.

And Harry? By the end of the term we had reduced him to skeletal bone and dried-out gristle. The lab assistants had removed his dissected body parts, and we were told they would be cremated in a non-denominational, religious ceremony.

We could not participate.

Once more I envy the present generation.

Hedley and Gable were unusually animated that second-to-last day lab day.

"Ladies and gentlemen, we have a rare treat for you," Gable trilled.

Uh-oh, she's getting another...

Shut up, Sal! She's one of the nicest people you could ever meet.

"Dr. Hedley has been experimenting with new and improved preservative fluids. These allow the body tissues to appear more normal, more ... uh ... lifelike in their flexibility."

In a flourish more appropriate to a *Cordon Bleu* Parisian chef, Hedley pulled the cover off of a small, wheeled table, and we stared at disembodied arms, legs, and heads that looked as though they had just fallen off someone walking by. He proudly picked up an arm-forearm-hand combination and pulled on the exposed tendons.

Those of you old enough to remember "The Addams Family" TV show may understand why some in our class began to laugh and clap, as Hedley the puppeteer manipulated that limb to move across the table. Then each of us experienced the *frisson* of shaking hands with it.

What about those heads?

If you are squeamish, skip the next paragraph.

Hedley took a flexible tube and inserted it into the stump of the trachea—the windpipe. He held the mouth of the disembodied head open and blew into the plastic pipe. An eerie "ahhhhhhh" resulted, as Hedley's breath activated the vocal cords of a dead man.

Congrats, kid. You didn't even flinch.

Thanks, Sal.

Time for me to go, Berto. You're gonna do just fine now.

Don't you want to see me make a fool of myself?

Nah, I know you won't. 'Sides, Corrado and I ... we're gonna have a gab fest with Harry and Shirley.

Good-bye, Sal.

Nope, it's arrivederci or ciao. See ya in ... oops—not supposed ta tell.

Sal ... Sal?

On the last lab day, Hedley and Gable congratulated us all for making it through the course. Gable had lost a considerable amount of weight over the year, and Hedley stood more and more at her side to steady her.

Gable, looking very tired, sat at her desk and smiled, as we all went to shake her hand and Hedley's. Then she gave her valedictory.

"You are my last class, ladies and gentlemen. I am, as the more astute of you already know, dying of a particular form of cancer. I want to let you know that I am donating my body upon death to this very lab. I know that John," she turned toward Hedley, "I know John has also made arrangements for himself.

"God bless you all."

Our first year was over … right?

Guess again.

Now we faced the dreaded week of comprehensives.

Our little black bags sat on the shelves in our dorm rooms. We sweated in Richmond's oppressive heat and humidity, as we pored over all of the notes we had taken during the past year.

Pass the comps and you moved on to second year; flunk and you were either out or—the greater ignominy—forced to repeat year one.

You know the sensation from hearing fingernails scraping a blackboard? (Do they still use blackboards?) By day seven of the comps we would have torn the head off a chicken if it looked at us sideways.

"You're breathing too loudly, City Boy."

"Do you know how annoying your nasal whistle is, Country Boy?"

It actually helped. After we wrestled each other to the floor, we sat there laughing. Then we hit the books again.

That final day, we turned in our last exam booklets and headed out.

Dave was going to spend two weeks at his family's farm before returning to his summer job at the school. I had a job lined up as well. It would be two whole weeks of doing nothing, hearing nothing.

"Wanna come home with me, City Boy?"

We left together.

Two weeks later we were back in the anatomy building. Dave and I worked as gofers for several graduate students, doing the scut work and bone articulations of skeletons for teaching assistants.

"Galen, Nash, would you guys wheel this over to the ENT lab in West Hospital?"

Charlie Nestor, our boss, was winding up his Ph.D. in human anatomy. His research had developed the new preservative fluids for lab specimens. He was pointing at a medium-sized, wheeled table with large, dark-plastic jars on each of its three shelves. It was surprisingly heavy and needed both of us to maneuver it through the streets. We looked like demented hot-dog vendors, dressed in foul-smelling, green lab smocks.

Two blocks and two elevator rides later, we reached the lab where the residents specializing in head-and-neck surgery honed their skills on cadaver specimens. The lab master signed our slips and helped us park the table along the wall.

As we headed out, we heard him laugh.

"Hey, guys, who's the joker who played makeup artist?"

We turned.

He had opened one of the jars and taken out its contents. It was a human head—hair combed and tied in a ribbon, wearing lipstick and facial makeup.

Gertrude Gable really did look natural.

Mother Nature Ain't Nice

"Holy shit!"

Andy Kagill clutched his groin protectively, while the rest of us guys experienced that uniquely male sensation that occurs when we sit in cold water.

The gals looked on with Mona Lisa smiles.

"Yes, ladies and gentlemen, this poor woman definitely had a vaginal overbite."

Second-year medical school had begun on a beautifully balmy, August day—definitely not weather conducive to studying. But this was pathology year, the year of the odd, the unusual, and the unexpected. Our previous year had been spent learning the normal, or what was considered normal. Now we got to see in full detail the tricks that Mother Nature could play on her children.

We stood there in the Pathology Museum, staring at a vast array of organ specimens in thick, glass jars. Needless to say, the urology and gynecology sections grabbed our attention.

"This is a perfect example of a teratoma," Professor Madden intoned, pointing at a large jar containing the mortal remains of a woman upon whom nature had bestowed the ultimate indignity: Lining her vulva were two complete rows of teeth.

For you scientifically inclined readers, teratomas are tumors that usually begin when a baby forms inside its mother. Cells that ultimately become different types of organs and tissues locate in the wrong place and develop just as they would in their correct position—hair, eyeballs, limbs, you name it. They can be found anywhere from the base of the tongue to the genitals.

Our class clown, Andy—yes, medical school has them—leered at his girlfriend, Tanya.

"You aren't going to surprise me, are you?"

The look on her face could have air-conditioned the room.

"You'll never know."

Most of us had survived the first year's comprehensive exams, that critical testing of mind and body, fighting fatigue and knowledge overload. Ten did not. Three would be repeating freshman year, one had shot himself, and six had decided their best interests lay elsewhere.

Year two meant pairing off, kindred men and women finding each other and beginning the dating/mating ritual full tilt. Dave had fallen head-over-country-boy heels in love with Connie, whom he called the Teacher. My other friend, Bill, aka Baby Face, had lost his gentleman's reserve over Peggy, the Southern Belle.

Me? I wasn't the passionate type.

Right.

Until I met June, aka the Model.

From that time on the six of us became life-long friends. We survived and thrived in school because of one another.

I miss you, my friends.

Sophomore year we carried our black bags to clinical presentations, ready to jump up and approach a patient staring back at us from a chair, wheelchair, or stretcher, when a professor called our name.

"Mr. Galen."

"Yes, sir?"

"Take a look at our patient. What are your observations?"

Dr. Stemp was known for pulling surprises.

The young man, no more than seventeen, smiled at me when I approached him. He sat in gym shorts and tee-shirt, totally unfazed by the two-hundred-or-so eyes staring at him.

"Hi ... uh ... Mr...."

"I'm Terry."

"Okay, Terry ... uh ... would you please take your shirt off?"

"Sure."

He reached over his shoulder and, in that special guy way pulled the back of the white tee up and over his head and then looked right at me.

I don't know if my classmates in the amphitheater saw it, but I had one of those pit-of-the-stomach reactions, when I spied the glistening, red-black, one-inch spot on Terry's right shoulder. I moved closer to him, palpated it, and then felt under his arms and around his neck. The enlarged lymph nodes were unmistakable.

"Terry, would you lie down?"

He stretched himself out on the cart, and I ran my fingers over the place in his abdomen where the liver would be. It wasn't hard to find. It was twice normal size.

I helped him sit back up and turned to the professor.

"Terry has melanoma, and it's spread to his lymph nodes and liver."

The room went silent. Even as sophomores we knew what it meant. We had just completed a section on malignancies of the skin. This young man's fate was sealed.

It is fairly easy to read a textbook and study photos and descriptions of different medical problems. It's another story when the subject is alive, alert, and damned nice.

"Didn't you forget something, Mr. Galen?"

Dr. Stemp raised his right eyebrow.

Terry whispered softly, so I think I was the only one to hear him.

"Listen to my chest, Doc."

I quickly opened my bag, took out my stethoscope, and self-consciously strained my ears. The classical machine-shop rumble of a hole in the heart wall separating the two main chambers roared back at me.

"Terry has a VSD, Dr. Stemp, a ventricular septal defect."

Stemp nodded, and I sat down.

In small groups, the rest of the class approached, examined the devil on Terry's shoulder, and listened to the demon in his chest. After we finished we applauded the young man, as an attendant wheeled him out of the room. When they reached the door, Terry sat up, forming the two fingers of his right hand in a V and yelling, "I'm going to lick this, guys!"

Stemp stared at the floor; the rest of us tried our best not to cry.

Other memories of those days march through my mind: more practical exams with microscope slides, unlabeled organs in jars, and fresh specimens delivered straight from the operating room or the morgue. Each bore the cryptic questions designed to tease and distract us. We didn't just identify, we had to extrapolate: What would you expect this patient's blood tests to show? What symptoms did he or she experience because this organ was not doing its job? And so on.

We learned something else: vigilance. At conferences we saw doctors called on the carpet and made to look like fools for missing what were obvious diagnoses to the pathologists, once they had sliced open a deceased's body. We witnessed even high-and-mighty specialists knocked down like bowling pins by the pathology reports. And indirectly we learned that cherished beliefs often have no basis in fact.

"Class, Mrs. Dayten was kind enough to share her problem with you today before her surgery."

The general surgeon smiled benignly at the middle-aged woman sitting in the wheel chair. We had just studied breast tissue and the various tumors that could occur.

"Miss Sabo, would you do the honors?"

My classmate Judy hesitated then rose from her seat and approached the woman.

"Hello, Mrs. Dayten, I'm Judy. What seems to be your problem?"

She jumped back reflexively when the woman abruptly pulled open the top of her gown. Even from the back row we could see the corrugated surface of her left chest.

Paget's disease of the breast. Insidious and misleading, it often appears as a skin rash like eczema and lulls the unaware into ignoring it until it becomes untreatable. Today's health-savvy women are trained not to ignore even the slightest changes. Back then, neither the patient nor the medical professional was as enlightened.

Once more we stood in small groups around our patient and saw and felt the *peau d'orange* (orange-peel) roughness of the skin over the tumor.

Mrs. Dayten was to undergo a radical mastectomy in several hours. The women in the class held her hand.

We knew what would happen to her. Surgeons would remove not only the entire breast but also the lymph nodes under her arm and even some of the muscle tissue. That side of her chest would become a living skeleton.

Now, decades later, I shake my head in dismay. The procedure maimed those who underwent it and did little to prolong their survival.

What present-day treatments will become anathema under the scrutiny of future knowledge?

The year progressed, and we marched through the various disciplines of the human body, studying each organ system with its unique chemistries, physiology, and anatomy, both visible and microscopic. And as we did so, we were introduced to the living personifications of what could go wrong.

"Note the dimensions of our patients' chests and the way they breathe."

We traveled by car to other institutions, including the local Veterans Administration hospital on the outskirts of Richmond. There we saw first-hand the ravages of lifetime smoking, compliments of the countless, free cartons of cigarettes given to soldiers during both world wars.

Two men, old before their time, sat in chairs, plastic tubes feeding oxygen from portable tanks into their mouths and noses. I stared at them—so different and yet so alike. One looked like he had just been rescued from a concentration camp: Thin and emaciated with flushed skin, his every attempt to breathe seemed a tiring effort. The other soldier, barrel-chested, wheezed and coughed and spat sputum (phlegm) into a cup by his side.

Seeing them took me back to my childhood, to my world in the tenements, when I was just a kid called Berto. To this day I retain vivid images of the Old Guys, three World War I vets who gathered at the shoe-repair shop of their legless war buddy, Harold Ruddy. That's where I saw the devastation caused by the Germans' use of mustard gas. Our neighbor, Tim Brown, lived a life of oxygen deprivation, drowning in a sea of air, because his lungs were almost nonexistent.

But the men in that veterans' hospital hadn't been gassed—at least not by others.

They had unknowingly damaged themselves with decades of heavy smoking.

"Class, note the typical 'blue-bloater' and 'pink-puffer' *habitus* (body shape) of our patients."

Dr. Marja Gortan was a lung specialist, a former refugee from Eastern Europe. Diminutive, almost doll-sized, she paced back and forth in front of us, her long, white, professor's coat fluttering, as she pointed out the skin color and body shape of the thin emphysema patient and the large-chested variation, which we then called chronic bronchitis. Now they are considered varieties of chronic obstructive pulmonary disease.

We walked through the respiratory patient ward wide-eyed. Men and women, so desperately ill from cancer that holes had to be cut in their necks, had tubes inserted to bypass the tumor-scarred upper parts of their windpipes. Such images burned themselves into my brain: Terminal lung and voice-box cancer patients, some with no vocal cords, were forced to speak by burping out words. And what were they doing? Inhaling cigarette smoke through those tubes, their wasted fingers shaking, while they held the lit cigarettes up to the openings in their necks called tracheostomies.

When we left the VA hospital to return to our campus, Dave looked toward a nearby doorway and gasped.

"Geez, looka' that!"

The six of us stared: Gortan was standing in the doorway lighting a cigarette.

Year two saw perverse cosmic jokes played by the Fates on the unsuspecting.

That year we lost our class clown.

"I have some tragic news," the dean announced. "There was a terrible auto accident this morning and . . . uh . . . Mr. Andrew Kagill was fatally injured."

He cringed, when a loud scream erupted from Tanya. Other students quickly surrounded her, and the sobs were not just from the girls.

This is life's biggest lesson: No one is immune to the Dark Angel.

But the bitter irony lay in what transpired later.

The year was coming to a close. We had covered the various internal pathologies of the human body, and now we would be exposed to the accidental.

"Old Gordie's gonna do the horror show, isn't he?"

Dave and I sat in the amphitheater next to Bill, June, Peggy, and Connie. The pairing was so obvious that no one laughed or made snide comments anymore. Our little group had found itself.

This was climactic, *Grand Guignol* horror show. Given by one of the foremost forensic pathologists in the nation, it was an anticipated event for every second-year class.

Gordon Makland had made a career of studying the effects of external trauma—accidental, malicious, or self-inflicted. Was it chance or murder? Show him a body, and within minutes he could tell you cause of death and whether or not it was by chance. He could wax poetic on the effects of gravity and its impact on falling bodies and why certain teenagers unintentionally killed themselves by hanging.

"Old Gordie's slide show," as everyone called it, was the culmination of our sophomore studies.

Makland was not one-dimensional. He was also an avid amateur geologist and rock hound. I was, in later years, privileged to accompany him and play mountain goat and spelunker in search of mineral specimens.

That day in late April we sat and fidgeted and nervously joked, while Sid Graham the projectionist set up the 35-millimeter slide trays. Yes, young doctors, we actually used primitive stuff like film back then.

Makland stood in typical slumped pose, his gaunt, six-foot-four frame leaning over the podium. He nervously drummed his fingers so close to the microphone that the room resounded with laughter to the elephant-herd noises. When he caught on and stopped, the dark-blue eyes in his rectangular, jowly face penetrated the semi-darkness, and he cleared his throat. Then he smoothed graying cowlicks back into place and harrumphed.

"I want to warn you, ladies and gentlemen. What you are about to see is graphic, raw, and not to be taken lightly. These were once living beings like you. If I hear any snide comments or levity I will end the session. I will also have the offending individual expelled. Do you understand?"

We all nodded.

The first slide startled all of us. The vacant-eyed face of a dead, motor-vehicle-accident victim stared back at us in full-frontal view. A good part of his brain had been forced down through his nose from the impact of his head against the windshield.

His demise had occurred long before mandatory seat belts and collapsible steering wheels.

"Visualize the force vectors involved as this man's head hit and penetrated the windshield at sixty miles per hour."

He didn't have to remind us—we could feel it.

Slide two: two bushel baskets containing what appeared to be pounds of raw hamburger. What seemed out of place was the foot still encased in a worn work boot poking out the top of one basket.

Makland's voice seemed overly dry, as he off-handedly remarked, "This farmer got pulled into his own thresher machine."

One student in the back rose and quickly ran out of the room.

Slides three and four. Front view: a small hole with burn marks in the middle of a young woman's forehead. Her eyes had popped out of their sockets. Back view: Most of her skull was missing.

"This was the result of domestic violence. Love and hate walk side-by-side, ladies and gentlemen. Please note how the shock wave of the bullet caused a massive exit wound."

Several more students rose and left.

And so it went: bodies turned to mush by falls; burn victims, their muscles so contracted by the heat that they appeared to be in a boxer's stance; drowning victims, their bodies bloated and their lips, earlobes, noses, and eyelids eaten away by fish and crabs.

"That should do it. You can shut down the projector, Mr. Graham."

The Fates laughed cruelly, as Graham's finger hit the advance button by mistake.

Along with gasps, we stared at one final picture. Taken through the passenger door, the view showed the auto-accident victim impaled by the steering post, legs pulped by the engine, mouth wide open, tongue protruding, eyes staring at eternity.

You would have become a fine doctor, Andy.

May brought the usual, early, Richmond summer heat and humidity, but we sweated more heavily for another reason. Now we faced the first of a three-part hurdle to achieve the degree of Doctor of Medicine: the first part of the National Board of Medical Examiners' certification exam. The faculty had lightened up on its academic onslaught by giving us review classes covering all of the information that had swamped us over the past two years.

Once again we cocooned ourselves in our rooms, hid out in library carrels, or found secret, unused niches in the education building to study like monks. Not even our friends could help us through this.

We had been warned that part one was written by Ph.D. types, so we had better know all our basic sciences. It has always been a running battle between the Ph.D.s in science and the M.D.s as to what really matters in a medical education. As students, we were caught in the middle of the academic fracas.

It took two days, and when it ended our fates were sealed. Those who passed would advance to year three. Those who did not either had to retake it or a state-sponsored, equivalent-competency test. Neither was a piece of cake. The prime advantage of passing the National Boards lay in one word: reciprocity. Those who successfully completed all three parts—the first now, the second at the end of year three, and the third during first-year post-graduate—would be granted a license to practice medicine in all but three states: Florida, California, and Hawaii.

The reason? Those three sunshine states did not want to be inundated by geezer physicians when they retired.

"Hey, City Boy, got your whites yet?"

Dave stood in the doorway of our apartment on Church Hill, looking like a thin line of whipped cream. He grinned at me. In one month we would be hitting the wards.

Soon our little black bags would be put to daily use.

I quickly changed into my outfit, and we laughed hysterically at our reflections in the full-length door mirror: tall and short, slim and stocky, Mutt and Jeff.

We changed back into civvies and ran down the stairs to Dave's car. Once more we headed to his family's farm near Lynchburg for some well-earned rest and relaxation.

We would need it.

Year three would use live ammunition.

Lock and Load

Berto, do you really want to be like me?

I lay in the four-poster, twin-size bed, the overstuffed mattress probably not much younger than the handmade, chestnut-wood frame passed down through six generations in Dave's family. The rustic sounds and scents easily penetrated the thin bedroom walls: crickets chirping, small nocturnal creatures rustling through piles of decaying leaves, the ch-hoot of the wood owl, and the groaning yips of raccoons competing for food scraps tossed atop a nearby compost pile.

Even the early summer couldn't ward off the natural night chill permeating the little farmhouse in the middle of nowhere. I settled the patchwork down quilt around my neck, turned on my side, and closed my eyes. It was so easy to fall asleep.

I dreamed that night.

I was once more a young boy named Berto. I strode through the alleys of my memory, seeing once more the friends who had shared my life: Angie, Tomas, Salvatore, and others. I ran through the tenement streets, legs pumping, breathing in short gasps in anticipation of what I would see, what I would learn next at the storefront clinic run by my mentor, Dr. Corrado Agnelli.

Doors seemed to melt away. I entered the examining room. A man lay on a table. He was gaunt, wasted, the sheet covering his body missing the outline of one leg. I saw my friend, the one who had opened the door to my life's work, lying there.

"Corrado, it's me, Berto. What's wrong?" I heard myself cry out.

The face staring up at me smiled wanly, and then tears flowed from the man I had sought to emulate.

"I'm dying, Berto. I will die alone."

He paused to catch a breath then stared into my soul.

"Berto, do you really want to be like me?"

I awoke screaming with Dave standing over me and shaking me.

Those three weeks, between the end of sophomore year and the beginning of our clinical rotations as third-year students, were painfully short.

Dave's parents had accepted me as a second son, a brother to their only child.

They instructed me in the ways of farming and how plants and animals really lived.

Dave and his father, Big Dave, laughed at my awkward attempts to cut and split firewood. I nearly amputated my left foot and smashed my toe from clumsy swings of axe and hammer. His mother, Mary, showed me what fresh vegetables looked like and how to prepare them. To my amazement they were actually edible, not the gray mucilage I was accustomed to from my mother's ethnic, iron-cauldron-cooked, "everything soup."

Dave and I walked and walked over rutted dirt roads, gazing at gentle-sloping hills dotted with tobacco patches and pastures of grazing cows. My skin easily burned in the full, Virginia summer sun.

"Why do you want to leave here, Dave?"

We sat on mounds of hay grass, with large, dried-tobacco leaves our only fans and protection against the midday gnats and blue-tail flies that populated the cow pastures.

A nearby black snake sunned itself, as Dave turned to me.

"Sometimes even paradise can be boring, City Boy."

He looked down for a second then faced me once more.

"'Sides, I got Connie waitin' fer me, and I betcha you ain't stopped thinkin' 'bout June."

Later we walked past the now-abandoned tin shack, where Aunt Hattie, the local conjer lady, had lived and died, and I felt once more the chill of my first and last encounter with the burnished-ebony woman, when she had warned me about the Bone Man. We walked through cow-patty-filled fields and over rock-strewn woods. Dave easily stepped over the moss-hidden stones, while I tried my best to avoid tripping and breaking my neck.

I laugh now, as I remember how unsuccessful I was at avoiding cow pies.

Suddenly we came upon a clearing in the midst of Jackson oaks, persimmon trees, and scrub vegetation. The ground rose and fell in short mounds and depressions unlike anything I had seen before.

Dave stood there, head bowed, eyes closed, and I suddenly understood: It was a cemetery, his family's final resting place. Six generations of pioneer farmers, each striving to earn a better life, had lived and died on that property. Someday Big Dave and Mary would lie there, too. Dave was the first in his family to achieve his level of education. He was also the last of his line—unless Connie would change that.

We walked and walked, and we shared each other's demons. And then it was time to go.

Strange, as we left the little farmhouse to return to Richmond, Dave's parents hugged me as they did their natural son. They were proud of us both.

The first morning back we dressed in our starched white pants and shirts. They felt stiff and rough, not like the synthetic-blend fabrics used today. We had received our list of clinical rotations in the campus mail. For the most part Dave and I shared the same, six-to-eight-week turns in the various medical and surgical services. Connie, Peggy, June, and Bill had also been matched with us.

It was only a short walk across the Marshall Street Viaduct from our apartment on Church Hill. It was 6:30 a.m., but the heat was already scorching, by the time we neared the hospital. Cars honked at us, and drivers waved. The locals knew we were the new medical kids, little black bags clutched in our hands, striding into our first day of ward duty.

"Galen, Nash, you're with me."

Our first boss was Joe Tremayne. As a first-year, post-graduate—we called them interns then—he was directly in charge of us newbies. It was not considered a fun job. Not only did he have to do his own work, he also had to diaper and change us during our first, critical rotation. Of course the resident over him felt the same way about interns. Tremayne himself was fresh out of school, full of book knowledge and undergraduate ward experience. But this was also his first day as a real doctor. And so it went up the pecking order, from first- to second- to third- and fourth-year students, all the way to chief resident and attending physician.

Pity the poor nurses who had to deal with all those large-but-fragile egos!

We learned quickly who the real bosses were: the floor nurses and nurse supervisors—and justifiably so. They were the patients' first line of defense against the incipient young Dr. Frankensteins, who wanted to diagnose and cure everything while in reality creating mayhem.

We started in learning about early morning rounds, the ritual procession of students, interns, residents, and professor/doctors going from patient to patient, reviewing each one's status, test results, and anything else the attending could throw at us to catch us off guard.

"Dr. Tremayne, what's Mr. Jacobs' renal status?"

Our intern flinched. He began to reach for the patient's chart, but Dr. Godfrey slapped his hand away.

"Tremayne, I asked you a question. I don't want you to read. Do you or do you not know your patient's lab numbers?"

It wasn't a fair question. Tremayne had just arrived that day. The resident tried to explain that but was stared down. Godfrey's smile was not friendly. He had snared a victim. He would have fun playing with this mouse.

Then the floor nurse saved the day.

"Dr. Godfrey, Mr. Jacobs' test results aren't back yet."

She stared at the pompous ass. She had been the floor nurse when his ears were still wet.

"Uh ... thank you, nurse," Godfrey mumbled then turned toward another bed. This time he directed his questions at the resident, who had actually dealt with the patient.

After rounds, our crew, minus Dr. Godfrey, sat in the doctors' lounge in back of the nursing station. The first-year resident glanced at Tremayne then directed his remarks to us and the senior medical students.

"Learn to expect the unexpected. Know who and what you're dealing with, and then be prepared. Need I say more?"

We shook our heads.

The rest of the morning we introduced ourselves to our assigned patients and then familiarized ourselves with their charts. But that time was not uninterrupted. Patients could be sent to our floor at any time, usually admitted from the emergency room after they had been evaluated for their complaints. Those determined to have major problems were routed to a general medical floor.

Dave got the first one.

"Mr. Nash, please see Mrs. Cassidy. She's a lol (little old lady) with dyspnea (shortness of breath) and leg pain. Work her up for CHF (congestive heart failure)."

Tremayne was a nice guy and, as it turned out, a good intern and resident who later specialized in gastroenterology. We kept in touch for decades, until his sudden and unexpected death at age fifty-five.

He had always believed in being physically fit. Ironic, but he died in his home exercise room.

Dave was perspiring, as he grabbed his bag from the shelf and headed down the hall to room 315. I could see the orderly pushing a now-empty gurney from the room. His patient had arrived and was in bed. The nurse assigned to her would be checking her information and taking her vital signs.

I have always maintained the greatest respect for nurses and, after witnessing how one had gone out of her way to save Tremayne's ass, I vowed never to interrupt them when they were doing their job. It earned me valuable brownie points.

Bag in hand I likewise headed down the hall. I wanted to get to know my patients, get a feel for their physical and mental condition. There's a difference between assessing medical information and developing empathy and understanding. Good doctors are well-versed in their technical skills; great doctors understand people.

Thank you, Corrado, for teaching me that distinction.

I walked into room 312. My first patient, Leroy Simpson, had been admitted three days earlier. From the scuttlebutt, he was something of a scalawag with the ladies and was now suffering the consequences of severe prostate infection. His condition warranted IV antibiotics.

Yes, young doctors, today you whip out your electronic pads and send an e-prescription order for a quinolone (very potent) antibiotic after determining the particular type of germ causing the problem. And, yes, if your patient doesn't have prescription insurance, he or she will bellyache until the cows come home about the cost—often up to ten dollars per pill.

Your patient will be better in a day or two but still hate your guts.

Back in my day those drugs didn't exist. We were stuck with pills that could not handle those infections, so we were forced to pump very toxic medications into patients' veins—or their butts, if it could be given intramuscularly.

Sometimes it took two weeks in the hospital, assuming the patient didn't suffer complications such as inflamed veins, massive skin rashes, blood clots, kidney or liver failure, or even sudden death.

And if they got better they hated your guts.

Plus ça change, plus c'est le même chose.

The more things change, the more they stay the same.

I stuck my head in the door and saw a nurse taking Simpson's blood pressure and temperature. She saw me, smiled, and then resumed what she was doing.

Never interrupt a nurse.

She finished and, barely avoiding Leroy's attempt to pat her rump, passed me in the doorway.

"Thanks for waiting, Galen."

She was younger than I was, just out of nursing school and, I have to admit, if I hadn't been totally smitten with June, I would have been tempted. I watched her an extra second or two, as she left the room.

Simpson leered at me then growled, "You can't have her, Doc, she's all mine."

I forgot to mention: Leroy Simpson was eighty-six.

And so it went, awkwardly at first, then with a bit of chutzpah and luck, I got to know my six patients. Leroy was the oldest; Barry Jackson, nineteen, was the youngest—and sickest. The boy had swallowed ethylene glycol (antifreeze) on a dare, and now his kidneys were shot. Our job was to attempt to stabilize him before transferring him to the renal unit, where he would undergo dialysis.

This was in the early days of treating kidney failure, several years before two brilliant surgeons—David Hume and Richard Lower—pioneered a kidney-transplant program at my school.

Barry didn't make it.

Next, medical conferences at lunch where you could eat all the sandwiches you could steal from the faculty table. The afternoon brought scut work, such as taking blood, checking test reports, and wrapping up with the intern and resident. My friends had all gotten new patients and had done their first workups. They congratulated me for not having to work too hard that day.

Tremayne heard it and snickered.

"Don't feel bad, Galen. In case you haven't heard you're on duty tonight."

Yes, I had drawn the short straw. I would work the night shift and not return home until the following evening. I turned to Dave, who understood.

"Yeah, I'll drop by with some fresh clothes and your shaving kit."

It was after midnight when I got my first patient workup: Johnny Mangan. Johnny was the friendly young boy with only half a skull because of tumor surgery. I got to know Johnny's hopes and dreams in that brief time between my examining him and his death several hours later.

The nurses brought me his untouched breakfast tray.

My friends and I made our bones on that first rotation in general medicine. We saw life snuffed out despite our efforts. And we carried those memories forward into our personal lives and careers.

Next stop: surgery. Bill, Dave, and I felt like we had joined the big boys' club, when we entered the surgeons' locker room and got to see the Kings of the Hospital in the altogether.

Not impressive.

They showed us how to change into scrub pants and shirts and put coverings on our shoes and heads.

It was not an enlightened time for women, so Connie, Peggy, and June were required to change in the nurses' locker room.

We learned that surgical rotations required an inhuman schedule. The surgeons started rounds at 5 a.m. before working long hours in the operating room and then doing post-surgery follow-ups on their patients in the clinics.

In recent times, various regulatory boards have declared that students and residents should *only* work an eighty-hour week. But back then you went on duty at dawn and went home the *following* day at 7 p.m.—if you were lucky—and then it started all over again.

Thirty-six on, twelve off was the rule.

"Are you snoring, Mr. Galen?"

I felt the rap of a bloody forceps on my gloved hand, as I stood for hours holding a retractor while trying to control my bladder.

But we did learn. We helped yank out diseased gall bladders and perforated appendixes. We heard and felt the snap, as the orthopedic surgeon would rebreak an improperly healing bone and pin the ends back together. We observed the chest surgeon use giant snippers to cut through ribs to get at a lung or heart.

"Mr. Packard, a thirty-six-year-old carpenter, is here today for pericardiectomy, Mr. Galen. What were his presenting symptoms?"

We stood around the bed of the African-American man just before he was to be prepped for surgery that would remove the sack that covered his heart. He had suffered an unusual complication from an infection called rheumatic fever as a child. As a result the case around his heart had become stiff and hard, preventing it from fully contracting and expanding. He couldn't walk or do the activities that most of us took for granted without rapidly tiring.

That's what we all thought.

And then...

"Holy Jesus, look at that!"

The chief surgical resident had completed the initial cutting and removal of two portions of ribs to expose the heart. The heavy chest retractors had spread the ribs even farther, and we crowded and craned our necks to see what we could see from our back-row vantage point.

"Isolation precautions, stat!" the surgeon yelled, as we six, lowly, third-year students wondered what the hell was going on.

The operating room nurse quickly herded us aside.

"It's tuberculosis. I've never seen anything like this!"

Today's CT and ultrasound scans would have forewarned the surgeon. But we had only simple chest x-rays, and they could not detect the problem.

Ezekiel Packard had had rheumatic fever. What no one realized was that he also had tuberculosis and, unlike most TB that affected the lungs and kidneys, his infection had settled in the heart sack, the pericardium. The cheesy, thick-white, tuberculosis infection caused the scarring.

Tuberculosis is very contagious and, like syphilis, was a big concern among healthcare personnel, who had to deal with unknown patient conditions.

They shooed us out of the operating room and told us to shower and change into fresh clothes—a fitting last day for surgical rotation.

We were happy to be back in whites again. Now we would be on call only every third night, with kids and little babies the beneficiaries of our developing skills.

"Children are not small adults. Remember that, ladies and gentlemen."

That bit of wisdom emanated from the pediatric resident just before the professor of the day strode onto the ward. We had heard about Herr Professor Doctor Guetlich, aka the Nazi.

I have never been certain if the nickname fit. What I do remember are two things:

1. A previous, third-year class member had suddenly stood up one day, clicked his heels together, and shouted, "*Sieg heil!*" As the story was

told, Guetlich snapped to attention and returned the salute. Apocrypha?

2. The professor's favorite expression was "*Die kinder ist* germ bags." Children are germ bags.

We had been warned: Expect to get sick at least once during pediatric rotation. I was lucky. Growing up in the tenements and hanging out at Dr. Agnelli's clinic had exposed me to an array of bugs my friends had never dreamed of. I was the only one who didn't develop some kind of viral infection.

These were the days before multiple vaccinations turned kids into pincushions by their second birthday. We were expected to have received all the UCHD (usual childhood diseases) before entering medical school. Oh, we still had to be vaccinated against smallpox, typhoid, tetanus, diphtheria, and polio. God bless him, Corrado Agnelli had administered those fun-filled shots to me using the thick stainless steel needles so common then.

The effect was profound. I wanted to crawl under my bed for a week, especially from the old-style typhoid shot. But a number of my classmates were not so lucky. Two of the guys came down with mumps and became sterile. In adult males the swelling is in the genitals, not the face, and the disease destroys the reproductive cells. One girl barely missed developing encephalitis (a brain infection) from chickenpox, even though her parents had told her she had had the disease in childhood.

My friends suffered several viral respiratory infections, before their immune systems could get up to speed.

I also learned that, in pediatrics, book smarts do not always go hand-in-hand with common sense.

We were paired off in the infant unit the first week. This time my partner was Chuck, a classmate I knew only in passing. He was smart and had done well in the classroom and on written exams. But there was something not quite right about Chuck.

"My God, go stop him! Go stop your partner!"

The nurse came running down the hall and almost yanked me off my feet. She was gibbering.

"He won't listen, he won't listen."

Chuck had been assigned the job of obtaining a blood sample from a month-old baby, who had been admitted to the infant unit with an unspecified infection.

Simple task.

It is fairly easy to obtain blood from older children and adults. Put a tourniquet around the arm, watch carefully as a vein pops up in the elbow crease and, *voila!* You get your blood sample.

Babies are different. They are like very old people, whose veins in their arms and forearms are deeply buried and inaccessible. Instead, babies have nice, juicy, scalp veins on either side of their heads.

Chuck was very good at taking tests and reasoning from point A to point B. If you needed blood from an arm, you put a tourniquet around the arm above the vein.

And if the patient is an infant? Chuck's reasoning was very logical: For a scalp vein, well, you place a tourniquet around—you guessed it—the baby's neck!

I stopped him just in time.

Chuck was advised to switch to a Ph.D. program, and he did well at it. Years later I heard that he taught comparative anatomy at a university and was made the faculty adviser for students who sought to enter the healthcare field.

Sometimes I saw miracles.

"Galen, she needs an exchange transfusion."

The pediatric chief resident possessed the Wisdom of Solomon. Stuart Zelany was an older man, an engineer who had finally found meaning in life by returning to school, obtaining his M.D. then specializing in what he loved best: children. He, like Agnelli, was a doctor's cializing in what he loved best: children. He, like Agnelli, was a doctor's role model, a resident who made you want to stay late and observe him, even when you weren't on call.

"Here's the scoop, guys," his deep voice rumbled.

He was, to us kids, the Old Man—he was over forty!

"This baby has ABO incompatibility, and its red blood cells are being chewed up by maternal antibody reaction."

It was one of those genetic, toss-of-the-dice situations. The blood type of the mother and her baby did not match. Enough of the non-matching cells had managed to cross over into the baby's circulation before birth, so a destructive process had begun that caused the baby's red blood cells to break apart.

Little Tyra, who was not quite one day old, wouldn't survive another twenty-four hours, unless...

Zelany, mesmerizing us with his calm, steady voice, pointed out the increasing jaundice (yellow skin) and swelling in little Tyra's face and abdomen. He had us obtain special blood samples for blood-typing and cross-matching. Then he demonstrated the technique of putting a catheter—a plastic tube—in the large vein in her belly button.

Slowly he removed some of the baby's damaged blood into a large, special syringe and then, oh-so-carefully, gave Tyra the new blood. For each small amount of bad blood removed, an equal amount of good blood replaced it. The biggest danger was trying to remove and replace too quickly. That would overload the baby's heart and cause it to fail.

To this day I can see Zelany's ham-hock-sized hands gently holding that little baby and crooning over and over, "It's okay, little one. It's going to be okay."

It took several hours. We stood, watched, helped when we could, and even prayed silently. We exhaled only when Zelany smiled and said "done."

Tyra became a grandmother forty years later.

Amazingly soon third year was coming to a close with our last rotation in obstetrics and gynecology.

June immediately demonstrated her uncanny ability with the young, pregnant women in the prenatal clinic. There was a light in her eyes whenever she had the opportunity to assist a resident or attending physician in the birth of a baby or the surgical correction of a woman's pelvic problem. It was obvious to the rest of us that the Model had found her calling.

Dave had no such interest.

"City Boy, I've helped birthing in too many horses and cows to want to do it all my life."

Bill's skill and empathy made him stand out, but, he, too, did not have the fever for OB/GYN work, and Peggy and Connie preferred general medicine and pediatrics.

Me? I also found great satisfaction in catching babies. June and I were the only students whom the residents allowed to perform simple deliveries on our own. It almost became a contest to see who could deliver the most vaginal (normal) births.

I would like to say that I let June win, but she beat me fair and square.

I probably would have followed June into an OB/GYN residency except for one incident.

"Mr. Galen, would you like to assist me?"

It was a singular honor. Dr. Tully, the department chairman, was dealing with what he called an unusual situation, and all the other residents were involved in other cases. June also had a full schedule.

By then I was an old hand at suiting up and performing the pre-op, surgical-scrub ritual of cleaning one's hands and forearms before being assisted by the scrub nurse into sterile gown, latex gloves, and face mask.

I entered the OR and was startled to see that the patient lying on the table was a child. According to her chart, Saranda was only eleven years old. But she had been raped by her older brother, and Mother Nature had played the cruelest trick by allowing this girl to physically mature earlier than normal.

A child was going to have a baby.

I looked at the department chairman, a distinguished OB/GYN, and he saw my look.

"Saranda has a problem, Galen. Her pelvis is too small to deliver naturally. We're going to have to do a C-section."

Caesarian section: a procedure involving opening the abdomen, lifting the uterus up, and opening it to extract the baby, which couldn't escape any other way without hurting itself or its mother.

As the young girl was being anesthetized, Tully whispered to me through his mask.

"There's a problem with the baby, Mr. Galen."

I held the retractors and helped mobilize the uterus. The surgeon's scalpel quickly made an opening.

There was an audible gasp from the entire operating team, as we stared at what came out.

Nature is not nice. It doesn't care what we want or expect. I saw a misshapen creature with very small head. Everything was wrong.

"Mr. Galen, God help us, it's a fetal monster."

No, this was not some horror or science-fiction movie. When the genetic dice are tossed, sometimes they come up craps.

The term fetal monster is used to describe a malformed, genetic mistake. It can take many forms and appearances. The one kind thing about such a situation is that the baby is either born dead or does not live more than a few moments.

Such was the case with Saranda's baby.

I decided then and there that obstetrics was not my field. Maybe June would have felt the same. I'll never know—and I never told her.

I can still hear Saranda's groggy voice, as she awoke out of the anesthesia.

"Can I hold my baby?"

We ended third year with a fun-filled review before taking part two of the National Boards. It was more clinical in nature this time, and our ward duty had really helped us prepare.

Bill and Peggy were off to visit her relatives—always an ominous sign for a single guy.

Connie and Dave spent a lot of time at her apartment while Peggy was away.

About June and me, let's just say old Berto was no slouch.

But that's another story.

Year four would be starting soon.

Good Death, Bad Death

"I hate hawks."

Dave looked at me, puzzled, his right eyebrow raised. It was truly comical, an expression that didn't fit his angular face and beanpole body.

"Okay, City Boy, what's your beef now?"

"I grew up in a neighborhood of predators, Country Boy. It was bad enough when we killed and maimed each other out of sheer frustration. But when someone—someone who hadn't lived through what we did—deliberately preyed on us, well, we considered it a form of cannibalism."

"Bob, look over there. What do you see?"

A hawk sat at the very top of a sycamore tree. Suddenly it swooped down and seconds later flew up again with something wriggling in its talons.

The wriggling soon stopped.

The sight made me feel sick. I looked at my roommate and attempted to duplicate his raised-eyebrow stare.

"That was the death of a living creature, Dave."

"That's right. Now, what would have happened if that critter, probably a field mouse, hadn't been snatched?"

"It would have lived out its life, had a family, and died of natural causes."

"What the hell are natural causes, Bob?"

"You're asking me that, Country Boy? You, especially, should know the answer. We get old. Our organs don't work as well. Somewhere along the way our body no longer functions as it should, and our heart stops."

"City Boy..."

He paused, his voice now reflective.

"Bob, haven't you ever had to put down an animal?"

"You mean...?"

"Yeah, something you kinda grew up with, petted, maybe milked or rode and loved in a way that only kids can love a pet."

I didn't answer. I stared ahead then closed my eyes, my shoulders slumped.

No, Dave, but I held too many dead or dying friends in my arms.

I couldn't have replied without sobbing.

"Okay, now tell me the difference between that mouse dying suddenly and quickly, or gradually deteriorating and becoming unable to run and find food? That's a prolonged death of starvation."

"So when your time comes, you want it quick and dirty, huh?"

He grinned.

"Yeah, preferably in bed with..."

Just then we heard Big Dave shouting at us, so we ran across the field to the little, white-clapboard farmhouse.

Dave rushed in ahead of me

We saw Big Dave holding Mary in his arms. She was shaking her head.

"It's nothin'. Jes' one o' my dizzy spells. Don't make sech a fuss, Pa."

She looked pale, almost gray, but she pushed her husband's arms away and sat on one of the handmade kitchen chairs nearby.

Dave looked plaintively at his mother and father.

"What happened, Pa?"

Big Dave was wringing his gnarled, work-hardened hands.

"I jes' stepped out fer a second, and when I came back in, yer ma was on the floor."

I glanced at Dave then walked to the little bedroom where I was staying to get my bag. Every time we returned home, Dave and I would bring our black bags. It made the two old folks so proud to see their "two boys," as they called us, walking in with them.

Big Dave had built three bedrooms onto his one-room bachelor house, when he and Mary had married. They had planned on a large family, but two years after Mary had Dave, she lost what would have been his kid brother shortly after birth. That third bedroom had remained empty, until Dave brought me home on my first visit. Now his folks called it "Bob's room."

"Yer not gonna doctor me, are ya, Bob?"

I laughed, trying to hide my concern.

She was still gray.

By then Dave had retrieved his own bag, and we pulled out our witchdoctor's gadgets, while Mary kept scolding us.

"Quit makin' sech a fuss!"

Dave wrapped a blood-pressure cuff around his mother's right arm, while I listened to her chest with my stethoscope. The sounds I heard were unmistakable. I waited until he finished, then we switched places, and I saw the recognition in his eyes.

Mary Nash had an irregular heartbeat typical of atrial fibrillation—the rapid, uneven beating of the small, upper chambers of the heart. Coupled with that was the harsh flow murmur of aortic regurgitation. The valve through which blood flowed from the big, left side of the heart into the aorta—the major artery of the body—was not closing fully.

"Ma, we need to get you to the hospital—now!"

She shook her head, and so did Big Dave.

"Son, if'n ah'm gonna die, it's gonna be here."

"Yer ma's right, boy."

No amount of talk or reasoning could sway them, so we stopped, put our bags back in our rooms, and went back outside.

"See what I mean, Bob? Do you understand now?"

I nodded.

"But I still hate hawks."

We left the next day. Our two-week vacation between junior and senior year had ended on an anxious note. Dave offered to stay and take care of his mother, but neither of his parents would hear of it.

"Now you git yer tail back to school, boy! Yer not gonna drop out jes' fer a foolish ol' woman with the vapors."

Mary Nash was short and thin, her face wrinkled before her time by hard work. But she was one powerful woman who knew what to say and why. She and Big Dave had watched their son grow into something previously considered unattainable by the family. She wouldn't let the specter of her own mortality stand in his way.

I drove the car down the rutted dirt road, as he craned his scrawny neck to get one last look at his parents standing and waving at us.

We drove back to Richmond in silence.

Four hours later we pulled into the parking lot of our row-house neighborhood on Church Hill. Dave went straight to his room. I picked up the mail, tossed out the junk, and paid the bills. Then I headed upstairs.

His door was closed, but I could hear his sobs. I raised my hand to knock but hesitated. Instead I went to my room and lay down. I decided to rest, just for a moment.

"Berto."

"Si, Mama?"

"Be very quiet. Your papa, he is sick."

I was twelve. Papa couldn't be sick. Papa was always strong, always well. Papa never cried, never complained. Oh, I saw him tired. I saw him upset, when stupid things were done at the foundry. But sick? No, my papa could never be sick.

I took my shoes off and tip-toed toward Mama and Papa's bedroom. In today's world of bloated mansions it wouldn't be large enough to be called a closet. But in our tenement apartment it was a bedroom. It was dark. That was not unusual. Electricity cost money. But this was daytime, and the window shade was pulled down.

Papa lay there on his back, head elevated by a pillow. What seemed like every few seconds his body would spasm with uncontrollable coughing. Sweat poured off his forehead, but he shook with chills.

I went to his bedside and whispered, "Papa, can I get you anything?"

The single moan from his dry lips scared me into running out of the room.

"Mama, I'm going to get Dr. Agnelli," I yelled, as I headed for the outside door.

I didn't wait for an answer. I forced my shoes on and donned the heaviest coat I had. It was unusually cold even for New Jersey in January. I ran down the three flights of stairs and out the front door, moving as fast as I could to the storefront clinic run by Dr. Corrado Agnelli.

"What's wrong, Berto?"

I was out of breath. I gasped, "Papa is sick."

He didn't hesitate. He grabbed his coat and reached down by his old desk to grab a large, black-leather bag.

"Come on, boy. Let's look at your papa."

Even running I could barely keep up with his stride. His long legs devoured the distance to our apartment and took the stairs two, sometimes three, at a time. He knocked, and Mama answered the door.

Dr. Agnelli headed right to Papa's bedroom and opened the shade.

I saw my father lying there, in full daylight, haggard and weak. I had never seen him like that.

Dr. Agnelli quickly examined him. Then he opened that magic bag of his and took out a syringe and a bottle of off-white liquid. I watched, as he cleaned the bottle top then stuck the needle into it and drew up a full dose.

"Antonio, turn over."

Mama helped Papa onto his right side, and I winced, as the big needle quickly entered his left buttock. Papa didn't move or say a word, but then he relaxed and seemed to go instantly to sleep.

Mama and I followed Dr. Agnelli out into the sitting room.

"Anna, he has pneumonia. I gave him some penicillin. We'll see how he does the next twenty-four hours. Just keep trying to feed him."

"*Dottore,* will my papa get better?"

I looked up at my role model, my eyes trying hard not to tear up.

I remember Corrado patting me on the head.

"*Si,* Berto. Your papa is a very strong man."

He was right. The next morning Papa was up and eating like nothing had happened. He smiled at me, actually smiled at me, and uttered two words.

"*Grazie,* Berto."

I smiled back … and awoke.

The sun was setting. It was after eight o'clock that July evening in Richmond, as I walked to Dave's room, knocked, and walked in uninvited. He was lying face down and didn't turn, until I said as softly as I could, "I know how you feel."

Dave snuffled, turned, wiped his eyes, and sat up.

"Come on, Country Boy. Let's see what we've got in the fridge."

We headed downstairs, and I fixed us a supper of canned soup. We shared some words and then went back to our rooms.

Senior year started in the morning.

Med school senior year—one of growing confidence and final decisions.

Once more we began the first day by walking across the Marshall Street Viaduct from our Church Hill apartment. Once more the early morning Richmond sun reflected off our whites—the pants-and-shirt combo worn by students on ward duty. But this time was different. We strode up the hill laughing and joking about who and what we would see and what strange cases would astound and confound us. No more upperclassmen now. *We* were the seniors!

That realization became especially pleasant, when we noticed the third-year kids milling in confusion at the entrance to West Hospital and then shared a knowing look.

Did we, could we, have ever looked like that?

Dave yelled out a, "Hey, don't sweat it. You'll get used to being eaten alive."

"Yeah," I threw in, "just take the time to make sure you don't taste good."

One girl looked quizzically at us. She was the only one courageous enough to ask, "What do you mean?"

Her friends laughed nervously, as we headed toward them. Dave smiled and said, "Just don't worry. It won't help, and all it does is encourage the bastards who enjoy seeing you sweat enjoy it more."

I nodded and repeated the advice our resident had given us the first day of last year.

"Always expect the unexpected. Always assume that they are out to get you. Remember, even paranoids can be right sometimes."

"Sandy, believe only half of what these two guys tell you."

Dave and I turned around at the voice behind us. June was smiling at me coyly and licking her lips.

"Stop by sometime, and we'll tell you the full scoop about these two—especially my Farm Boy."

Connie was with her, now standing on tip-toe and patting Dave on the head. Bill and Peggy, as suited a southern gentleman and his Southern Belle, stood back and just smiled.

Dave's face matched the rising sun on a stormy day. Mine was not much lighter. But we hugged our friends and fairly danced with excitement.

The A Team, as we had begun to call ourselves, was together again!

Senior year is a year of electives: Take one from column A and two from column B; a Chinese smorgasbord of different rotations, from which everyone could pick and choose.

By senior year we were expected to have formed a pretty good idea where our medical degrees were steering us. The masochists who loved surgery could enjoy it to the max by taking rotations in everything from general to open-heart to ear/eye/nose/throat. Those who enjoyed surgery, but didn't like to get their hands dirty, could gravitate toward anesthesiology.

The crowd that liked kids could specialize in pediatrics, adolescent medicine, or any of the areas, from pediatric infectious diseases to rehabilitation therapy for injured and maimed kids, that fell into the category.

As for anatomy, we had two major options there: radiology, for those who naturally saw the hidden details in shadows, and pathology, for those who could fit fleshy puzzle pieces together to make a diagnosis.

And, for those who entertained their personal demons, what better pigeon hole than psychiatry?

So it went. All of us had matched together on three different medical rotations. Then the luck of the draw sent Dave into an intensive-care stint, while I manned the medical-emergency room. The following month we would switch places.

June had filled the latter part of her fourth year with obstetrics and gynecology. That was no surprise. She was a natural at it. I lucked out in doing one of the OB/GYN rotations with her. In retrospect, I wish I hadn't.

"Hey, you two, we got a direct admission coming through Surge' ER. She's Dr. Tomlinson's patient. Therapeutic D and C for DUB. Oh, and don't get lost in the tunnels, understand?"

Dr. Maggie Tronell, our resident, winked at June, who smiled noncommittally.

What the hell had she told Maggie?

One of the staff gynecologists, a Dr. Tomlinson, was admitting his private patient to the special deluxe floor for wealthy patients who suffered from what we commonly called "female problems." Our patient was being admitted with a diagnosis of dysfunctional uterine bleeding—DUB. Strictly speaking that meant she was having heavy, irregular periods. Tomlinson was going to do a dilatation and curettage—a scraping procedure to remove the overactive lining in her uterus to be sure there was no malignancy.

June looked at the admitting sheet.

"Bob, she's only twenty-two!"

We shared a suspicious look.

Usually D and C was done on older women, and usually only after a trial of hormone treatment to attempt to chemically cause the lining to slough off. We didn't see any notation of that having been done.

I bowed to June's superior knowledge and asked the big question.

"Then why…?"

"I've got a bad feeling about this one. Let's see if they did a pregnancy test on her."

It wasn't there.

We both turned to Maggie, but June had the *cojones* to ask, quietly, "What's going on?"

Maggie Tronell was a bit older than the other residents. She had been an army nurse before going back to school to get her M.D. She closed her eyes and shook a head covered in dusty-gray hair.

"Are you two that naïve?"

In fact, we were. This was another time, almost another world from the one we live in today. *Roe versus Wade* was still in the distant future, and deliberate abortion was considered illegal, immoral, and every other bad word you can think of.

Yes, there were exceptions, where the life of the mother was considered at imminent risk. But in Virginia, a legal abortion could be performed only if a committee of doctors and lawyers presided over by a judge permitted it.

I make no moral judgment either way. My entry into the world of medicine was arranged by a dead girl, killed by a backroom abortionist when I was eight years old.

June and I also manned the OB/GYN pregnancy clinic, where busloads of scared, barely teenage, poor-and-pregnant girls were brought in to have their babies delivered in facilities that were old when our grandparents were born. The faces of those kids—and that's what they were—lying on their backs, moaning in agony, and being given inadequate pain medication, because we didn't have enough, remain vivid in my mind.

And, there was a flip side. There always is.

In the OB/GYN clinic it was not unusual to see one patient who was the proverbial Mother Hubbard, who had so many children—you know how it goes—and then see a desperate couple who could not conceive no matter how hard they tried.

"June, why can't we match these two groups together in some informal adoption arrangement?"

Talk about naïve. Another resident overheard me and verbally ripped my head off.

June remained silent, until the resident asked if she agreed with me.

"Why not?" she replied.

I think we spoiled that guy's day.

The third side? That was what we were now going to learn.

Maggie took us into the residents' lounge—actually a converted closet—and sat us down.

"Listen, kids, the world ain't fair. You know that."

Dear God, yes, I knew it well, even then. My old neighborhood would have turned Maggie's hair grayer than it was.

"Here's how it works. Now, don't interrupt me, young lady!"

June was rising to protest, but I put my hand on her arm, and she sat down.

Maggie's eyes were tired now. What unimaginable things had this woman seen in war?

"You two know that legal abortions are as rare as hen's teeth, but legalities never stop people with money. That's a fact. You understand? Now, go and escort our patient to the floor."

We nodded, stood up, and walked out quietly.

June kept silent by biting her lip.

I started to say something then didn't. This was one time when my stupid gene mercifully didn't assert itself.

We walked through the connecting tunnels in silence to the surgical emergency room. There were private anterooms that served as holding areas for patients who were bypassing the ER to be directly admitted.

Our patient was young, a lot younger than twenty-two. She reminded me of my Marigold Lady, the dead girl who had found me in the river. A slender build capped by golden hair and green eyes, her face was well-known in the local papers as the daughter of a prominent Virginia state senator. She was scared.

June tried to break the ice, as we entered the room and closed the door.

"Hi, I'm June Ross, and this is Bob Galen. We're here to escort you upstairs. How are you feeling?"

What broke was a flood of tears and a desperate moaning, "I want to keep my baby!"

June and I both averted our gaze. Whether it was anger at what was happening, or shame at what was going to happen to this girl, I'm still not sure.

"Can't I just go home?"

She stared at us with pleading eyes.

"How old are you, Christine?"

June was looking at the birth date on the chart, and it didn't fit.

"I … I'm seventeen. I'll be eighteen tomorrow."

June sat down, and I followed suit. Now we were both smiling. She took the girl's hands and held them.

"Chrissie, do you have any friends you could stay with overnight?"

"I don't under…"

Then a light lit up those beautiful green eyes.

"Yes … yes, I do!"

For the first time she smiled, and June and I returned the favor.

"Now listen carefully," I whispered. "We want you to leave quietly and go to where you know you'll be safe. June and I will have to pretend to shout at you to come back, but don't turn, don't pay any attention. Just keep going."

I reached in my side pocket. I only had a dollar on me, but I gave it to her.

June looked at me as she never had before. It felt good.

Christine hugged us both and moved toward the door.

"Slow, don't run. Don't attract any attention to yourself. We'll start to make some noise after you get outside," June added, as our patient started to open the door.

We saw Christine exit the big glass doors of the ER.

June closed the anteroom door then kissed me. She whispered, "I didn't know bears had feelings."

We walked leisurely back through the tunnels to Maggie.

She did not look happy.

"Where's the patient?"

"She changed her mind," we answered in unison.

Maggie shook her head.

"What did you two do?"

"She turns eighteen tomorrow," June said. "She'll be able to make her own decision then."

June held my hand.

"Girl, you don't know what you've done! You don't know this kid's father. He'll do whatever's necessary—no matter how old she is!"

With that Maggie turned and walked away.

I was scheduled to be on call that night, but June stayed with me. She even brought me dinner. For a while, things were quiet, and then the duty nurse paged me.

"A patient of Dr. Tomlinson's is being sent up for an emergency D and C. Do a quick pre-op check on her as soon as she hits the floor. Her name is Christine..."

June rose from her chair at the name, and we both felt the same chill shoot up our spines.

The attendant pushed the gurney cart out of the elevator and steered it toward Room 3. June and I ran and saw the young woman lying there with her eyes half-lidded. She had been drugged.

A voice from behind startled us. It was Maggie. Her face was creased. Was it sorrow, sympathy, pity?

"I warned you. You don't know this girl's father."

"Maggie..."

June started to cry, and Maggie put her arms around her.

"The senator's personal physician gave her a shot of phenobarb after they caught her," she whispered.

Maggie turned to me.

"Do you want to scrub in?"

I declined.

I made rounds then held June's hand, until the nurse called me to the recovery room.

That night, Christine died of post-operative hemorrhaging and anesthesia complications. Time of death was 11:59 p.m..

Things were never quite the same between June and me after that. She seemed to withdraw and focus on her work, but at the same time she became needier. To the male mind, it was a contradiction, a conundrum—just plain screwy.

An old man looks back and understands—but only to the extent that a man can truly fathom the other half of the human species. My fun-loving, brilliant, independent June was steeped in guilt—as was I. Would Christine have lived, if we had not interfered?

The young me saw only the young woman. June saw the young woman and the child within. No man can truly understand that. No man can truly understand the anger and disgust directed both externally and internally over what another man—a father more interested in his career—could have done to his daughter.

In my own bumbling way, I tried to refill that void, that loss of confidence in June. Then, my stupid gene took over.

"Dave, I'm going to ask June to marry me, but I want to get her the best ring I can. I'm going to take on that externship in the Detox unit at night. I think I'll have enough by May to buy it. Then I'll propose just before graduation. Whaddya think?"

Yeah, guys talk, too, and not always about sex. Dave and I had become de facto brothers even in the eyes of his family. I knew that he was totally hooked on Connie and had similar plans in mind.

As for Bill and Peggy, that was just about a done deal. Bill also spoke of a graduation proposal and marriage.

But what those two guys seemed to know instinctively, and what I was totally clueless about, was this: The one you love wants and needs your attention. It makes no difference why you are not there when she needs you.

Dave looked at me and asked me the question that I was too stupid to comprehend.

"Bob, how are you going to spend time with June if you're working double shifts?"

I didn't hear him. All I could imagine was June being overwhelmed by my sacrifice to get her a ring.

That May, I stood in her apartment, ring box in my pocket, and I popped the question.

That damned ring still sits in its box in my desk drawer over half a century later.

The six of us graduated on a beautiful day in May. One couldn't ask for better weather. The sun was shining, the temperature slightly cool and dry for a Richmond spring.

I saw the senator standing next to the university chancellor and the dean of the medical school. He was doing his best to get into as many photos as possible.

As I said, I hate hawks.

If It Ain't Broke

"Code Blue! Code Blue! Surgical recovery suite 3."

I sat bolt upright in the house-staff, on-call room. No thought, no hesitation.

Four years of Pavlovian training summoned me.

It was my first year of post-graduate internship.

I raced down the hall to where it seemed half the hospital staff had crowded into that little room.

Crash carts.

Sounds of chest compression.

Calls of "Stand clear!"

The discharge of the defibrillator paddles.

Ozone mixed with the sweat of multiple doctors and nurses.

And a near-lifeless body rising and falling in galvanic response.

The boy was young, probably nine or ten. He looked like he had been playing with his father's shaving cream. Pink froth covered the front of his face and poured out of his mouth and nose with every chest compression performed by the resuscitation team.

His condition: massive pulmonary edema (fluid in the lungs) from heart failure.

They worked on him for forty minutes. No electrical response on the monitor.

The chief resident shook his head.

"Let's call it. Time of death..."

I heard the nurses sobbing.

"What happened, Kathy?"

The young nurse leaned against the wall, clenching and unclenching her hands. I held her until the sobbing stopped. Then we left for the nursing lounge, where we sat down.

"That poor kid—he didn't need to be here. His damned parents wanted him to have his tonsils out. All the other kids in their neighborhood had had them out. But he didn't need it!"

The boy had slipped into heart failure from an unusual response to some of the medications used during the procedure.

The law of unintended consequences: If it ain't broke, don't fix it. Or, in medical parlance: First, do no harm.

I'm ashamed to admit I don't remember the boy's name. I'm not sure I ever knew it. Or maybe my old-man's memory has granted me forgetfulness. But it took a while. For a long time, after I started my medical practice, the image of that little body lying motionless on the hospital bed stayed locked in my mind.

"What's the schedule look like, Barbara?"

I crossed my fingers. It had been a busy week in the office.

"We got us a bunch of worried well."

I sighed. Chest pains, high blood pressure, even bladder infections were preferable. Dealing with a patient's self-image is the hardest job. I do not envy the psychiatrists or the cosmetic surgeons.

Jack Collins was my first patient that morning.

"Hey, Doc, you're looking good!"

Jack was six feet tall and one-hundred-eighty pounds of muscle. Life had no meaning for him, unless he worked out at least four hours a day.

"You, too, Jack. What can I do for you?"

"I'm not right, Doc. I eat only healthy foods, do my workouts, and still I get colds. Besides, I'm the puniest guy at the gym."

Jack could easily lift me with one hand and pitch me across the room. He reminded me of my boyhood friend, Sal.

"Come on, Doc. Look at me! I'm a weakling. Don't you have something to bulk me up? I talked with my trainer and he suggested..."

I listened. It was the usual bad advice about pills, shots, and dietary supplements. By themselves, not bad, but when taken in the doses his trainer wanted, Jack would slip into kidney and liver failure in no time.

The real question was, why? Why was Jack so driven to bulk up?

I held up a mirror.

"Jack, what do you see?"

"One puny son of a beeswax, Doc."

When I examined him, on the surface he looked damned good. But I had learned that doctors can be fooled. So I ordered some lab tests that focused on body metabolism, and I managed to persuade him, temporarily, to hold off on doing anything drastic. I still didn't know what I would tell him if—and when—the test results came back normal.

But other events intervened.

One of Jack's trainers had begun injecting him with illegal steroids, and they definitely bulked him up. They also made him very volatile. Eventually the police arrested Jack for beating up his girlfriend. They called it 'roid rage.

Six patients with colds and backaches, then...

"Come on back, Mrs. Filman."

Betty Filman was thirty, a good-looking young woman with auburn hair, bright blue eyes, and a full figure. She surprised me with the first words out of her mouth.

"I want to have breast implants, Dr. Galen. I need a pre-surgical clearance."

Trust me, Betty Filman needed breast implants as much as I did.

"Why, Mrs. Filman? From what I see, God has already blessed you with beauty and a great figure. Other women would kill to look like you."

Okay, I'm not the most subtle of physicians.

"Bill wants me to have it done."

Bill Filman was an up-and-comer in the business world. To hear him tell it the world revolved around him. Keeping his wife in trophy shape would validate that perception. And unfortunately, in Bill's world, trophy shape meant she needed "big bazookas," as Thomas, my old neighborhood barber, used to say.

"Are you sure? Your husband should count himself one lucky guy to have married you. You don't need to do this."

"Yes, I do, because he'll love me ... more."

She stared at the floor.

I saw the fear on her face, and I heard the unspoken thought: Bill was looking for greener pastures. So I completed the required, pre-surgical exam.

Psychologists call it Body Dysmorphic Syndrome, or BDS. We all suffer some degree of anxiety about our looks—how we appear, how we stack up against the other guy or gal. Ask a teenage male what's the first thing he looks at in a locker room. He won't admit it, but you already know, because you did it yourself. Size matters, and so do looks, strength, and all of the other physical attributes that keep the human race dating and mating.

We remain members of the animal kingdom, competing for the most desired mate or the most powerful position in the pecking order. We lie awake at night and stare in our mind's mirror at the unwanted hair loss and color changes, and the deterioration of skin and muscle tone.

Sometimes that anxiety grows extreme, so gnawing that it becomes obsession—it becomes dangerous and self-destructive. We fixate on the unnoticeable spot, the slight crook of the nose. We enrich the plastic surgeons—and justifiably so—for their skills in disguising the ravages of age.

Betty Filman had her breast implants. The lily was gilded.

Bill Filman divorced her three months later.

Another type of demon can lodge inside us, one that makes even the BDS patient seem normal.

"Dr. Galen, my daughter won't eat."

Lavinia Baker sat across from me. Her daughter, Cassandra, sat beside her, almost invisible, physically and emotionally.

Cassie had turned fourteen three months earlier. Always slender, with a pleasant, rounded face, the Cassie I saw that day startled me. Her formerly natural, wavy-brown hair looked stringy and dull. She had combed it down over her wan face. Brilliant brown eyes now sat flat and sunken, as if part of a death mask.

"Mrs. Baker, why didn't you call me earlier?"

"I didn't think anything was wrong. I mean, Doctor, I was worried about my weight at her age. All her friends are model-slim. My husband even used to crack jokes about Cassie's baby face making her look fat."

I closed my eyes. There are times when I have to resist the urge to jump up and throttle the person talking to me.

Mrs. Baker did not realize it, but her daughter Cassie was slowly dying. Her condition achieves the same mortality statistics as certain cancers: *anorexia nervosa.*

Yes, it does affect young women more, but men aren't immune.

To the anorexic patient all mirror images are distorted into the circus-fun-house illusion of the morbidly obese. The tall and slender perceive themselves as bowling-ball fat. Food becomes the enemy, obsessed over, never out of mind. Eating must be avoided. If the urge overwhelms, then they take laxatives or diuretics, or they self-induce vomiting (*bulimia*) to correct the perceived problem.

"Mrs. Baker, I'm afraid Cassie needs to be hospitalized immediately."

"Can't you just give her some pills or a shot to make her eat?"

"That doesn't work, Mrs. Baker. Remember Karen Carpenter?"

The lead singer of the singing group The Carpenters had developed *anorexia,* and the condition led to her death at age 32 of heart failure.

"But Cassie's not crazy."

"Neither was Karen Carpenter. We don't know why this happens. We have done all sorts of research on the changes in brain chemicals that occur in adolescence. All we have learned is that there is no simple answer.

"Cassie needs to be hospitalized, worked up for correctable problems, and then intensely monitored and counseled. She needs to have her food intake watched and measured. She needs to be placed where she can no longer do things to compound the weight loss."

"I don't think my husband will agree to that."

I stared at her for a moment.

"Then Cassie will die."

She stared back at me.

"Come on, Cassie. Let's find a doctor who knows what he's doing."

The girl hadn't said a word. She just peered at me with one eye through the hair *burka* covering her face.

"What's eating them?" Barbara asked, as she walked into my office after mother and daughter had left.

My secretary could always get right to the point.

"It's who's not eating, and that wasn't a worried-well patient."

"Yeah, my bad, Doctor. What's her problem?"

As I recited the litany on *anorexia,* Barbara shook her head.

"That mama won't listen."

"Neither will her father."

I called Social Services. They informed me that they couldn't (read "wouldn't") get involved.

I called Cassie's school. Same response.

Cassie's father hung up on me.

Four months passed. I was about to sit down with Cathy for a Thanksgiving dinner she had prepared from scratch. She was a great cook.

The phone rang.

"Do you have to answer it, Tony?"

I smiled. She already knew the answer.

"Dr. Galen?"

"Yes?"

I could hear loud noises and shouts in the background.

"This is Sergeant Janly with county rescue. You got a patient, Cassandra Baker?"

"I'm not sure she's my patient, Sergeant. Mrs. Baker left my office very upset some time ago, when I told her that Cassie was anorexic."

"Do you know if she's been seeing another doctor?"

"No, I don't. What's the problem?"

"Parents found her in the bathroom."

"Was she vomiting?"

"Looked like it."

"She's…?"

"Yeah."

Cartoonist Walt Kelly once imbued his lovable but species-indeterminate, comic-strip character Pogo with a bit of wisdom for the ages:

"We have met the enemy, and he is us."

ICD 798.I

Even the Dark Angel has a number.

"Dr. Galen, I think you'd better take this call."

My secretary was always right.

"Bob, Mary's gone! My Mary's..."

Big Dave's voice dissolved in tears.

I waited until he caught his breath then asked him what I already knew.

"What happened?"

"Bob, we were eatin' breakfast, and Mary got up ta check th' coffee pot, and she jes' ... she jes' had a droppin' spell. I tried what you boys tol' me ta do, but 't'weren't no use."

I could envision it happening: the sudden, irregular heartbeat brought on by Mary's damaged heart valve, the loss of consciousness as the blood flow to her brain dropped, and then the fatal, irreversible heart rhythm that took her.

I felt cold. Rationally I had known it was going to happen—that it would have happened even if Dave and I had been there. But the loss, the never-ending loss, it overwhelms reason, and the irrational grief takes over.

"Big Dave, have you called Dave?"

"N-n-no, Bob. I figgerrd I cud reach you better."

"Okay, I'll call him. You stay with Mary. I'll call the sheriff as well."

I was two years out of residency. It was before rescue squads and fast-response ambulances emerged, especially in rural Virginia. The sheriff's department would notify the coroner and, under the circumstances, the appropriate people would reach the little farm in due time.

Meanwhile, Big Dave would need that last bit of togetherness with Mary.

I wiped my eyes and dialed the Florida number I knew by heart.

"Dr. Nash's office, how may I help you?"

"It's Dr. Galen. This is an emergency call."

"Yes, sir, please hold."

Seconds later, I heard the familiar country twang.

"Hey, City Boy, what's the problem? Finally lose your virginity?"

"Dave, it's . . . it's your ma."

I could hear his gulping breaths. He knew, even without asking. It's the curse of those of us who understand the human condition.

I kept on talking; I didn't know what else to do.

"I called the sheriff's office, Dave. They'll get someone out there."

"Dad?"

"He's with her. Do you want me to make the arrangements?"

I could hear him sobbing. I waited until he whispered, "No, I'll do it."

Mary Nash had survived almost six years after that first episode the summer before senior med year. She had lived and died on her own terms. Here one second, gone the next. It's called Sudden Death Syndrome, and in the International Classification of Disease lexicon it's ICD 798.1. No prolonged stays in hospital or nursing home, and no tubes and wires inserted while families hover over shallow-breathing, almost-corpses.

The year seemed filled with them.

I had inherited some patients from an elderly doctor who literally died with his boots on. They found him sitting at his desk, his pen hand poised over a patient's chart, when the Dark Angel called on him.

Still grieving, his wife had phoned me and asked if I would accept his patients. Her parting words to me were that he had considered them family, and she couldn't rest until she knew they would be cared for.

I was young then, and sentimentality was not a word that would have described me. But I liked old Doc Benton, so I agreed.

That's how I met Clarence and Clotilde Culbertson.

I remember my first house call to the stately home of that amazing couple. It was located in an upscale Virginia suburb near Washington. I stared at the autographed, ancient photographs of them, scattered about in silver frames, posing with notables such as Enrico Caruso and Cosima Liszt. And I marveled at the personally dedicated paintings by famous French impressionists that adorned their walls.

Clarence and Clotilde had passed their century mark by the time I first saw them. Clarence was descended from a wealthy family, the typical second son who did not inherit the family fortune but still had more money then he needed. So, what did he do? He became an explorer, one of those latter-third-of-the-nineteenth—yes, nineteenth—century world travelers and big-game hunters, who went everywhere and did everything. Most of us can only use our imaginations, when we read about such folks in the penny dreadfuls of that gilded age.

"Young doctor, ever see elephant tusks? How about African water buffalo?"

I stared at the mounted heads along the walls of Clarence's study, above photos of the young Culbertson standing over each of his kills.

"See that tiger, boy? He killed forty villagers, before I brought him down. Got to like the taste of humans. Probably couldn't catch any real game. Know why?"

I stared at the striped head mounted on a teakwood plaque. The taxidermist had posed it open-mouthed

"Yes, sir, I do. It had bad teeth."

"Bravo, bravo! I see you are a true diagnostician. Now, can you tell me how that tiger got its revenge on old Culbertson?"

I stared at the old man. One hundred years does a lot to people, but I took a wild guess.

"You caught malaria."

"Damned straight, boy! Had the *aiguë* for weeks. Drank quinine water till my tongue wanted to fall out, but here I am."

We laughed, as I attempted not to cringe. That poor tiger! Dave had been right about the field mouse.

Clarence had come of age in a time when J.P. Morgan and other robber-baron princes ruled the world and its high society. His family was part of that social milieu, and that is where he met the beautiful Clotilde Mayson, inheritress of wealth equal to the Culbertsons. While Clarence sought adventure overseas, Clotilde's musical talent had earned her a reputation as a piano prodigy by age sixteen.

Soon Clarence and Clotilde's antics filled the restrained gossip columns of the day. Even old Joe Pulitzer's scandal-rag newspapers were kind to the wunderkind couple. Their marriage was the talk of high society, and their guest lists could fill today's history books.

Clotilde once showed me a fabulous machine she called an "Edison." It looked like the top of the old treadle sewing machines the women had used back in my tenement neighborhood. She carefully removed the curved, wooden cover, took a black cylinder—which I later learned was made of wax—and placed it on the horizontal spindle. The house man (They employed a cadre of maids and butlers.) carefully attached a morning-glory-shaped horn to the gadget, wound the crank, and a Liszt piano mazurka came forth in room-filling volume. Clotilde's hundred-year-old, water-sapphire eyes glistened, as she told me, "Doctor, I was twenty when Mr. Edison recorded my playing."

Their home soon became familiar to me—even its smells of furniture polish and dusty damask, which seem to pervade all museums and old homes of the wealthy.

Dare I say it felt strange? After all, here I was, now grown up but still a product of the New Jersey slums, walking through the home of two living legends.

When the Culbertsons accepted me as their doctor, I became part of their standing guest list, invited for dinner and entertainment, after opening my little black bag and waving my witchdoctor rattles while pronouncing them healthier than the majority of the human race.

Did I say entertainment? That's too mild a term. Imagine a production by the cherubim and seraphim. Dear Clotilde never lost her talent, even as she passed her *cent'anni* milestone. She would take her seat in front of the great, thick-legged, antique, concert-grand piano, a gift from Kaiser Wilhelm II of Germany.

"Oh, yes, my dear, I can still hear old Willie harrumphing, his withered left arm twitching in my face. Never thought he would become the black sheep of Europe."

She attempted an exaggerated, heavy-German accent to imitate the Kaiser. And she would click her heels together, just as he must have done in his high Prussian boots.

"Yah, in de-e-e-e-p appreziashun fur helping Frau Wagner with the Bayreuth Festival."

Yes, she was talking about the wife of Richard Wagner, albeit of a common-law marriage.

On the evening of Clarence and Clotilde's one-hundred-first birthday—the Fates had even bestowed on them the same natal day—they once again invited me to drop by for a house call, dinner, conversation, and the music of the spheres.

We arose from the ornately carved, teak dinner table and entered the salon—a room no proper, nineteenth-century household would be caught without. The air of aging, hardwood bookcases, and that strange scent of decay emanating from the heavy, brocaded curtains still waft in my mind.

Clarence and I took our seats, as did the maid, the cook, and the butler, on leather-covered, high-backed, mahogany chairs. We applauded, as the grande dame made her entrance.

Of the two centenarians, Clarence was slightly the worse for wear. His exposure to foreign climes and bouts with tropical diseases had taken their toll on his skin and looks.

But Clotilde, still straight-backed and regal in pose and poise, sat gracefully at the keyboard. She turned her aquiline face toward us and smiled. Her eyes still glowed intensely. Her voice, untouched by time, carried that distinct, refined, nasal tonality produced by Manhattan's upper-crust society. It sparkled with laughter, as she addressed the little audience assembled before her.

"Ladies and gentlemen, Dr. Galen, my beloved Clarence, tonight's selection will be a medley. See if you can guess the names."

I will never forget the power of her performance! I can still see those porcelain fingers flying over the yellowed, ivory keys—keys that were the only earthly remains of some long-dead elephant that roamed the African savanna in the time of Bismarck and Tolstoy. And I was twice startled to realize that the pianist had emerged in the same era.

The magnificent music of Brahms, Chopin, and Wagner echoed through that salon. As Clotilde played, eyes closed in ecstasy, her body swaying in tempo, her sotto-voce humming barely audible to my young ears.

Her skin, translucent from time-lost layers of fat tissue, made her arms look like praying mantis limbs floating up and down the keyboard. Her feet feathered the three pedals to nuance the musicality of the notes.

Suddenly it was over.

We sat there, entranced by the virtuoso performance of this singular woman.

She rose from the piano bench and bowed to our rapt applause. I imagined her going through the same motions at New York's Old Carnegie Hall. She looked out beyond us, maybe seeing those great, past audiences granting her the triumph she so justly deserved.

Then she gazed down at Clarence, put her right hand to her lips, blew him a kiss—and died!

Even in death, her stage exit was one of grace and class. Her lithe body slowly folded in on itself and sunk to the floor, the pale, antique-blue gown she had worn settling like an open flower around her.

I was much younger then; I didn't understand.

I jumped from my seat and rushed to her body, mentally ticking off how I would proceed with cardiac resuscitation. But as I reached her and knelt beside her, I felt a powerful grip on my right shoulder and a voice which would have credited a man fifty years younger.

"Doctor, don't."

I looked up to see Clarence standing by me. He shook his head, and I stood up. His gray eyes flashed with the energy that must have dazzled his social set a century before.

"Let her have her stage exit."

I backed away.

He knelt down beside her, talking to her as he must have done when he wooed her. He stroked her silver hair and moved her hands together in prayerful repose.

All these years later I can still hear him repeating, over and over, those final words.

"Wonderful performance, my dear! Wonderful performance, Tillie!"

Then, almost in slow motion, his body folded over hers—and he died!

Several days after that strange and morbidly wonderful, final performance, I visited the local funeral home, which had laid out Clarence and Clotilde. There they were, side by side, just as they had been in life.

In those days I made it a point to pay my respects to deceased patients and their families. I entered the candlelit viewing room, moved up the aisle past the mounds of cloyingly sweet-scented flowers, and stood next to the twin biers.

I must admit, when I'm a spectator to these occasions, I find myself thinking what anyone else would: They really did look natural.

I closed my eyes and bowed my head in a moment of silent tribute. Then I looked up, alerted to the sound of someone approaching me: their sole-surviving grandson.

He put his arm on my shoulder and, in a voice more appropriate to a carnival barker, actually yelled out, "Everyone, I want you to meet Dr. Galen. He helped Grandma and Grandpa get to where they are today."

For a brief moment the viewing room grew deathly quiet. Then the sound of stifled snickers arose among the other guests. Quickly it crescendoed into guffaws and even drew the attention of the unctuous mortuary director, who joined the laughter when he heard what had been said.

To be fair, Clarence Culbertson III loudly proclaimed that what he meant was not what he said. But I resolved never to attend wakes again.

Mostly I have kept my resolve.

But little did I know what lay ahead.

The Newbie

"Doc, can we talk?"

The haunting notes of Grieg's "The Last Spring" had been drifting through my waiting room that blessedly quiet, late-spring day. I was thinking maybe I could relax a bit. But the young man slowly making his way up the walk erased that hope.

"What can I do for you, Rick?"

How many times had I said those very words? How many people had passed through my door to sit in that very room while waiting to be examined?

The shy, fragile, homeschooled boy I had first seen as a baby two decades before had blossomed into a tall, muscular, pre-med student. Now he was following the path taken by his grandfather almost forty years before.

His grandfather. Yes, I had first met the young ambulance driver/EMT in the emergency room back then, when he had wheeled in a snakebite case. Now, he was Dr. Richard Shepland, and Rick III was my patient, preparing to follow his grandpa—and me—along the Via Dolorosa of medical school.

"Dr. Galen, you and Gramps have seen and done so much in your life. Why did you decide to become a doctor?"

"Are you having a crisis of faith, Rick?"

Hey, if the clergy can say that, why can't I?

He laughed, but I saw the haunted look in his eyes.

I stared at the wall. My mind conjured up that life-changing moment in my childhood, when my Marigold Lady's dead hand beckoned me toward the river where she lay. Her unspoken words echoed in my mind.

Don't leave me!

I turned back to Rick.

"Like everything else in my life, a lady conned me into it."

I noticed that Barbara was about to speak up.

"More likely the devil made him do it, and that's not the whole story," she said. "The lady was dead—floating in the river—and he was eight years old. Told you he was weird, didn't I?"

My secretary was her usual, charming self.

"Well, Barbara, if I had told this young man that I found a coupon on the back of a Captain Marvel comic book, would he have believed me?"

"Comic book?" Rick asked.

"Yeah," Barbara snorted. "It said you could make easy money in your spare time with their little doctor kit. You didn't think he went to medical school, did you?"

I watched his reaction. Now he was truly confused.

"She's right, Rick. The lady was dead. But I have to give credit to one man, a true sage, who saw a wide-eyed, eight-year-old boy and became my mentor."

My other secretary, Virginia, had arrived, and she seemed stunned by what I had just said—I had never mentioned it before.

"Anybody we know?"

"No, his name was Corrado Agnelli. He was my guardian angel, my role model—more than my parents. He shared my dream. Even more important, he showed me wisdom…"

My eyes filmed over, as Corrado's uniquely accented voice echoed in my mind.

"Berto, come over here. Take a look at this!"

By the time I was thirteen I had become a constant visitor to the storefront, free clinic run by the immigrant doctor.

"I don't see anything wrong, *Dottore*."

"Look at the baby again, Berto. See anything unusual?"

"Uh . . . no sir."

"Ah, Berto, learn to observe with your mind as well as your eyes. You see a baby lying here. It has two arms, two legs, and two feet. You automatically assume that everything else is normal."

He held up the baby's right leg.

"How many toes, boy?"

I stared at the tiny foot.

"Geez, there's six toes!"

"Six toes."

"What did you say, Dr. Galen?"

Rick had risen from his chair during my reverie.

"Boy, the one thing my mentor pounded into me was never to assume something is true or normal just because you expect it to be so."

He stood silently for a few seconds.

"Dr. G., what was it like when you first started out in practice?"

"I was the typical new kid on the block. Thank God the older, established docs were empathetic to newbies like me."

When I was just beginning my practice, I would often visit patients in the hospital and make rounds with some of the med students. One day it was lunchtime, and my stomach was demanding sustenance in its own, uniquely vocal manner. I quickly scribbled some discharge notes for an elderly patient who had recovered from pneumonia, checked my bag to be sure I hadn't left anything behind in the patients' rooms, and headed toward the stairway down to the cafeteria.

That's when I heard a familiar voice.

"Hey, kid, wanna get something to eat? Our treat!"

I turned to see the Three.

Even now, decades after they had retired and gone the way of all mortal flesh, the mention of the trio of doctors still evokes nods and smiles from those old enough to remember.

Nelson Bolganich, George Maitland, and Joe Grasso.

White-haired, with piercing blue eyes that seemed out of place on that pudgy little body, Nelson had served in the Navy during World War II before joining the Public Health Service. Afterward he had opened a general medical practice in what was then a rural Virginia suburb of Washington. Roly-poly friendly, he could pin you to the wall, if you said something medically stupid.

George, husky-big, with basketball-player hands, and a former member of the Army Air Corps, had that lilting voice that always made you feel welcome—but God help the med student or resident who treated his patients in a blasé manner. George had no tolerance for sloppy or indifferent patient care. He also could verbally dissect a colleague who performed beneath his high standards.

Joe, "the Godfather," was balding and plump. He played the "Larry" to the other two stooges. A quiet, retired Army colonel and deep thinker, he could become an angry Vesuvius, when hospital staff members and ancillary personnel mistreated their patients. But he would open his wallet at the drop of a hat, if a nurse, medical student, or colleague fell upon hard times.

The three men had gravitated toward one another as kindred spirits.

"Come on, Galen, move it. Damn, even with my bad leg I can take the stairs quicker than you!"

Nelson had received a Purple Heart for war injuries, and by golly he could still take the stairs two at a time. He was approaching sixty then.

George, a young fifty-five, deliberately held back. His long legs would have left the other two—and me—in the dust.

Joe, the oldest at sixty-six, talked a mile a minute about the students, interns, and residents. Education was his life. Then he surprised me by asking for my opinion about the training programs and the quality of the new staff coming on board.

I hesitated, reminding him that I was almost as green as they were. Then his face erupted in a—to clean up the expression—pie-eating grin.

"That's why I'm asking you, Galen. The three of us are too old to remember how young flesh thinks."

Nelson and George countered with a "speak for yourself, geezer," just as we entered the cafeteria.

We grabbed our trays and moved down the counter, picking out entrees for the wait staff to place on them. I was hungry, but the stew of the day seemed to warn me away, so I snatched up two Jell-o cups, a banana, and what my city-kid sensibilities could barely accept as a roll.

Nelson laughed, as he asked for a double helping of what was euphemistically labeled pastrami.

"That's a biscuit, boy. Didn't they have biscuits where you grew up?"

Nelson, I never told you then, but no, we didn't have biscuits in my old neighborhood. What we had we were thankful for having.

George went for the fried chicken, and Joe selected a salted-pork dish.

I wonder even now: Nelson and George ultimately died from heart attacks; Joe tragically had multiple strokes, which whittled away at that wonderful mind of his.

Genetics or diet? Nature or nurture?

We sat at a round table—three knights and a squire—and once more I felt the scrutiny that only medical students and residents experience when in the presence of senior physicians. They bombarded me with questions about different medical conditions and how I would handle them. I knew I was being tested. And then it stopped.

The three lit into their food, while I managed to spoon Jell-o into my dry mouth and suck out the contents of an overripe banana from its skin. As I munched on the biscuit, Nelson looked up at me from the gray goo on his plate.

"Anyone croak in your charge, Galen?"

"Not yet. But give me a chance. I'm sure I'll do something right soon enough."

The other two laughed, and Nelson almost choked on his food.

"Come to think of it, guys, I had an interesting case a coupla weeks ago," George interjected.

"Yeah, this fella comes in complaining that the tip of his nose and chin hurt every time he made love to his wife."

"You sure he knew what he was doing?"

Joe's face had split into a grin, and even I had to smile at that one.

"Hold on, guys, we don't want to upset the kid here. Remember, he's still wet behind the ears."

Nelson looked at me intently, spooned more of the pastrami slop into his mouth, and asked the sixty-four-dollar question.

"Okay, Galen, what's wrong with Maitland's patient?"

I wondered why they were goading me like this, but I put the biscuit down and stared at each of them.

"You want a differential diagnosis?"

Now all three were staring back at me, and I felt the mist of sweat forming in my scalp.

The diff, as we called it, is a list, in order of likelihood, of what a doctor thinks is wrong with a patient. Usually the physician has a few bits of data and observation at his or her fingertips. Then they get swirled around in the little gray cells, eliminating some possibilities and raising others. But George had only provided that one, small, tantalizing bit of information.

Why are they testing me?

"Okay," I began, "your man is exercising rather vigorously, I assume, so two possibilities arise. One, he has a neurologic problem affecting the nerve endings that give sensation to his nose and chin. But that doesn't quite fit a defined nerve pathway, and if his brain had a problem in the area that recognizes faces, there would be other signs and symptoms."

The Three didn't take their eyes off me.

"Gentlemen, I've never seen a case like this, but I do remember reading about unusual signs of angina."

They all smiled!

Yes, to all of you would-be medical detectives, sometimes the only symptom of a potential heart attack is pain at the tip of the nose or chin—or even the tip of one finger on the left hand.

"How am I doing?" I asked George.

He clapped his hands.

"What happened to your patient?"

He frowned.

"I called Pat Boland and asked him to test the guy."

Boland was the best cardiologist in the area at the time.

"And...?"

"The guy leaves my office to go over to Pat's place ... and then he drops dead in the parking lot!"

Speaking of dropping, that's what my jaw did. I could barely get out a, "What did you do?"

Joe took the cue without missing a beat.

"He probably went outside, took the guy's wallet, and turned him around to make it look like he was coming in."

I noticed that Shepland seemed riveted to what I was saying. I think my story had scared him.

"Dr. Galen, why would those three doctors pull a joke like that on you?"

"It was their way of testing the new kid. They wanted to see what I could do and how I handled stress."

"But that doesn't seem fair, Doc."

"No one said that life was fair, Rick. And it did one very important thing for me. They asked me to join their on-call group. That was a great privilege and honor."

The young man exhaled. Then his face lit up.

"Did you ever actually have someone die like that here?"

"That's another story, Rick, and I probably don't have the time to tell it today."

"He's got the time," Virginia piped up, and Barbara nodded agreement.

Danged secretaries!

But then the office phone rang.

"You've got a busload of nuns with venereal disease coming in," Virginia said with a wink.

"Okay, Rick, I've gotta get back to work. Any more questions?."

"Yeah, Doc. Do you think I can do it ... I mean ... become a doctor like you and Gramps?"

"Rick, your grandfather asked me the same question forty years ago. Now, scoot, boy!"

"See ya, Doc."

What Goes Around

"Is this Robert Galen?"

When my phone rang that early May evening, I answered it in the usual, pleasant manner that has endeared me to so many of my patients.

"Who the hell is this?"

"Uh ... is ... is this Robert Galen?"

Once more my charming personality responded.

"Yeah, whaddaya want?"

"This is J.G. Traywick. Remember me?"

How could I forget? It was only ten years—ten years to the month, that last month of medical school.

Berto, follow your heart. Let no one—teacher, friend, even your parents—destroy your dream.

Corrado Agnelli's words had helped carry me through four, hard years of study. And a few weeks before those years drew to a close, the Powers That Be, representing none other than Dean J.G. Traywick, called us from our various ward duties to gather in the central amphitheater used for hospital lectures. They told us to expect something special.

By then our student black bags had become a bit worn. Sometimes the zippers stuck. On some the leather cracked. They had been scarred by use and abuse—as had we.

We were told to line up alphabetically. Those at the front had sneaked peeks through the doorway of the convocation room and passed the word back: "They're here!"

Our graduation gifts—full-sized, textured-leather, black bags with hinge flaps and our own names in gold lettering! When I received mine, I just kept staring at those thirteen gold letters: ROBERT GALEN M.D.

Ever since I was eight years old, when I discovered the dead lady in the river and first met Corrado, I had dreamt of this moment.

But I wasn't there just yet.

"Okay, Cinderellas, back to work!"

Traywick liked to think he had a sense of humor.

No matter. On our way back to Ward 3, Dave and I clutched our new bags, now rewrapped. Three more weeks and those two last letters would become fact.

I had night call. Every doctor dreads the middle-of-the-night, emergency-room admissions no one else wants: elderly nursing home patients, alcoholics in terminal liver failure, and others fitting no specific description.

It was 4 a.m. and, wonder of wonders, the place had remained quiet. I was checking on the patients unlucky enough to be there, but we had escaped the hassle of a new arrival—or, at least, that's what I thought.

"Mr. Galen, you've got one."

I cringed, as I heard the floor nurse called my name.

Soon I was standing over Eulah Jackson, eighty-six years old, African-American female, limbs contracted by stroke and poor nursing-home care, buttocks burrowed with pressure ulcers. Her head turned in the direction of my voice, as I introduced myself.

Eulah was blind.

"Let me go!"

It was barely a whisper, but I heard it.

I looked at her input record: strokes, heart attacks, infected ulcers, kidney failure, and blindness. Then, at the bottom of the page:

Lab shows probable acute multiple myeloma with secondary hypercalcemia.

She had fulminant, bone-marrow cancer with lethal levels of calcium, causing shutdown of bowel function and severe abdominal pain. If the poor woman had sneezed too hard her bones would have broken.

I worked her up, started some of the therapy required to lower her calcium to relieve the pain, and waited for the attending physician to arrive.

That event occurred at 6, when I presented my patient. The attending doctor elaborated an extensive treatment protocol, as the other students and house staff—and I—grew more and more incredulous. He was demanding treatment that was futile and absurd. The woman was ready to meet her Maker.

The intern and resident stared at their shoes. Even the nurses shook their heads but kept their mouths shut.

"Doctor Tinsley ... uh ... how will this help Mrs. Jackson?"

Yes, I opened my big mouth. Why would that surprise you? But I was confused. On the one hand I wanted to save the world. On the other my own life experience in the tenements told me such an ambition was futile. I had really just hoped Tinsley would aim me in the right direction, as had my mentor Corrado.

What I got instead was a piercing stare.

End of discussion.

Later, as I was getting ready to go for a quick lunch, the intern gave me a two-finger summons.

"The dean wants to see you."

Minutes later I sat in his secretary's anteroom waiting for an audience with the Great One. Normally friendly and talkative, she would not look me in the eye. Her intercom buzzed, and she directed me to enter the inner sanctum.

John Gilbert Traywick IV, dean, sat behind his double-size, dark-cherry desk. There was no doubt he was a scion of one of the school's royal families. There also was no doubt he fully intended to remind me of my own, lowly status.

"Sit down, Galen."

I was sweating in my starched student whites. He looked me over with his sky-blue eyes hooded by bushy-white brows. The jowls he proudly displayed in wide-faced smiles for publicity photos were now double-folded and scowling.

"Mr. Galen, do you know why I called you here?"

"No, sir."

"Don't you understand what you did?"

"No, sir."

"Are you stupid, Mr. Galen?"

"No, sir."

"But you just don't get it, do you?"

"Sir?"

His famous, exasperated look splayed across his face. He shook his head, but not one white hair moved.

"Mr. Galen, you showed great disrespect for your attending."

That thoroughly confused me. My grades were exemplary and my clinical work was never faulted.

For some reason a quote from the great Mexican general Zapata crossed my mind.

Moriría más bien la posición que vive en rodillas!

It's better to die on your feet than live on your knees.

I stood up, approached his desk, looked him straight in the eye, and said quietly, "Dean Traywick, I truly don't understand. What did I do wrong?"

I think I startled him, because he involuntarily pushed his chair back from his desk.

A few seconds passed. Then he resumed his position. I retreated and sat back down.

"Mr. Galen, why did you question Dr. Tinsley's treatment plan for your patient?"

Ah, so that was it! I cleared my throat.

"Sir, my patient is dying. She wants to die. What Dr. Tinsley ordered us to do was not in her best interest."

I knew it—I had crossed the Rubicon—but I was in it now, so I quickly continued.

"I appreciate Dr. Tinsley's expertise and skills, and I know I'm still just a student. But he must know—and have—reasons that I do not understand, so I asked him why."

Traywick stood up and faced me.

"Mr Galen, if you were any other student I would have expelled you. Do you understand that?"

"No, sir, I don't."

"Galen, you are living proof that education does not always convey common sense."

I had nothing to lose.

"Dr. Traywick, maybe you could…"

"God help us, you just don't get it. Get out of my office!"

I left and went back to the ward.

Eulah was lucky. She died before the testing could begin.

So was I, because I managed to graduate.

Yes, Traywick, I remember you.

"Uh … Dr. Galen, are you still there?"

"Sure."

"As you may know, I've retired as dean, and the alumni association has appointed me head of their fundraising committee. That's why I'm calling. As a graduate I'm sure you can understand the expenses of running the medical school and the need for support from our distinguished alumni. How much can we count on you to contribute?"

"Nothing."

"I'm sorry I didn't hear that. Guess I'm getting old. How much did you say?"

"Zero. Nothing."

"I don't understand."

"Mr. Traywick, are you that stupid?"

"Uh . . . I. . ."

"Well, J.G., I guess you just don't get it, do you?"

I hung up the phone. Dare I say that I slept very well that night?

Little Orphan Annie had it right: Tomorrow is only a day away.

I was nearing the end of another fun-filled, full schedule of patients: colicky babies, dyspeptic politicians, and a few chest and belly pains thrown in for good measure. I was beginning to run out of steam.

"Who's left, Virginia?"

I could sense my secretary characteristically raising an eyebrow.

"New patients, the Delauncys. She's coming in for a prenatal checkup."

I closed my eyes and rubbed my temples. Not my most favorite thing, seeing new patients at the end of the day.

I watched them out the window, walking up the sidewalk to the door, a couple in their mid-thirties, well-dressed with a confident stride.

Husband and wife sat together in the examining room, while I went through my routine questioning. Eric Delauncy was a professor of electrical engineering, and his wife Natalie was a graduate education professor. She explained that she was about four months pregnant—with her first child—and she wanted a mini-checkup before proceeding to an obstetrician. She noted that her cycles had stopped a little more than four months before.

She had no complaints and took no medication, but she did take vitamins and extra folic acid. She said she had read about their importance during pregnancy.

Her husband remained in the room at my request. I have always found it wise to do so, because a spouse's presence eases some of the nervousness for a new patient during an initial visit.

The examination was exceptionally unexceptional. Mrs. Delauncy was in excellent condition.

There was only one problem: She wasn't pregnant.

As I examined her, I became more and more convinced that what the young woman considered a pregnancy was actually an enlargement of the muscular lining of the uterus—a fibroid tumor.

Fibroids are not malignant, but they can grow to massive size.

As I completed the exam, I mentally rehearsed what I would tell the couple. After all, they both were highly educated people, and I was sure they would understand what I was about to discuss with them.

I began my spiel by emphasizing how well the general examination had gone, and then I explained my reasoning and recommendations about the fibroid.

I suggested two very simple things. One was a home pregnancy test—something Mrs. Delauncy had neglected to do. The other was an ultrasound image of the uterus.

But as I mentioned the word "fibroid," I could see the couple's pupils dilating. Frowns crossed perspiring foreheads, as I continued.

Suddenly, husband and wife stood up in unison and walked out of the examining room. They remained tight-lipped silent, hustling past my secretary and out of the office.

"What did you say to those two?"

Virginia was as stunned as I was.

"The truth."

Two weeks later I learned from one of their friends that the couple was very upset at me for claiming that Mrs. Delauncy was not pregnant. As the messenger of that information had put it, I was—in their eyes—the "tool of the devil and the spawn of Satan" for even suggesting such a terrible thing.

"Way to go, Galen. I've been telling everyone that you're a bit strange."

Jeff Schulman was both a knowledgeable and empathetic OB/GYN with my patients, so I bounced the situation off his brain cells in the hospital cafeteria a few days later.

"Be careful, Jeff. If the Delauncys are right, just think what the tool of the devil and the spawn of Satan can do to you."

"Yeah, you can talk me to death."

We laughed and finished our sandwiches.

By the time a whole month had gone by I had put the episode out of my mind. At that point in my life I had come to realize that I couldn't please everyone. I only hoped that the couple had found someone else who could satisfy their needs.

As I tried to catch up on some paperwork, Virginia yelled from the reception room, "Dr. Schulman's on the phone."

"Bob, guess who I just got called to see in the emergency room?"

Jeff had been summoned by the ER physician to see a patient suffering severe hemorrhaging from her uterus. He had to perform emergency surgery to remove a sixteen-pound fibroid that had outgrown its blood supply and torn a blood vessel.

"Wow, sixteen pounds! That's big," I exclaimed.

"Yeah, and she still doesn't believe it."

Uh-oh! Now I knew why he was calling.

"Jeff, are we talking about...?"

"You got it."

Poor woman, I thought. Now she knows for sure. I felt sorry for her and her husband—until Jeff added, "And let me tell you, the De-Launcys are really pissed off at you."

"Me?"

"Strangest damned thing, Galen, the two of them kept repeating your name. I heard the wife say you were the tool of the devil and the spawn of Satan, and that you had changed her baby into a fibroid."

I hung up, as Jeff laughed his head off.

I sat at my desk and stared at the wall.

Maybe you were right, J.G.

I picked up the phone and dialed information.

Three minutes later I heard the old man's voice.

"Traywick, this is Galen. Put me down for..."

Higher education does not convey common sense.

Dealing with the human condition does.

.25 Caliber

"Doc, the condom broke."

I answered the phone on the first ring and stared, near-sightedly, at the glowing dial on the clock radio at my bedside: 2:30 a.m.

One of the blessings of being the son of Antonio Gallini is the automatic on-switch I inherited from Papa. He never needed an alarm clock to awaken at any desired hour of the night. Besides, we couldn't afford one.

"Yes, Chet, and...?"

Another genetic characteristic gave me immediate voice recognition.

"Katie's pregnant, Doc."

I admit I was stunned.

"Doc, did you hear what I said? Katie's pregnant."

"Well ... congratulations, Daddy."

Chet Kamtow was one of my young patients. I had followed his development from a scrawny, withdrawn kid into a smart-and-savvy young man, someone who was embarking on the same path that had enticed me. He would be heading off to medical school in a few months.

It was my privilege to be his sounding board, a sympathetic ear sharing the milestones—joyful and awful alike—of Chet's life. One of the mixed blessings of knowing and following patients over decades was that they often told me first about their college and career hopes, and the rollercoaster maelstrom of their love lives.

So it was with Chet. When he fell head-over-heels in love with Katherine Howard, my phone would ring at many an odd hour, whereupon the young man would relate his attempts to cope with the emotional flood of the mating ritual. And now that ritual appeared to have reached a crescendo.

"Doc, she's amazing. She's ... uh ... she's got it all. You know what I mean?"

Why do the young always assume they are the first to experience love?

"We're gonna get married on Monday!"

Fair enough. Chet had always been a standup kind of kid, very focused, with a strong sense of responsibility for his actions. Besides, he and Katherine were totally in love, and it would have happened sooner or later.

We exchanged a few more words, and then I hung up. As I attempted to go back to sleep, I stared up at the shelf opposite my bed. On it sat a stuffed toy dog and a few other, tangible memories of my past. I wondered what my own present and future would have been, had the Fates not intervened.

Once more the phone rang. It was 3:15 a.m.

"Dr. Galen, this is Sergeant Bachlick of the Fairfax County Police Department. Is Justin Mowbrey your patient?"

Yes, he was—another promising young man.

"What happened?"

My skin started to crawl.

"He shot himself."

"Is he...?"

I waited an eternal second for the response.

"No, we've got him here in the ER. Shot himself in the shoulder."

"I'll be right over."

Medical school trains you to do things at warp speed: eating, dressing, and all the little personal tasks in which normal humans like to luxuriate, such as hot showers.

Only military people do it faster.

I was out the door at 3:25.

I drove in the predawn darkness, car headlights bouncing up and down with each road rut and turn. The racing engine played background to my racing thoughts.

Justin Mowbrey. Not quite nineteen. College freshman.

He was relatively new to my practice. A brilliant kid with an underlying sadness that I couldn't fathom, he seemed to have everything going for him: brains, good looks, athletic build, and a quick wit that could put the late Johnny Carson to shame. I had no doubt he would succumb to the dark side and become a lawyer.

What worried me was the emotional monkey on his back—hidden, yet coloring everything he did.

I pulled into the medical staff's parking lot and pushed open the ER doors. My ID badge and my face got me a wave-through from the guard, who threw in a friendly, "Hi, Doc."

I didn't have to ask where to go. The trauma team had crowded into Bay 3. I stayed clear, until an opening appeared, and then I stuck my head in.

Justin lay naked on the gurney, IVs inserted into his left forearm, an intracath in his left neck. His veins were swallowing bags of blood. The front of his right shoulder was hamburger.

"He yours?"

Jake Turner, the trauma-team captain, turned toward me, his scrubs blood-soaked.

"Yeah, what happened?"

"Shot himself. Cops say a campus security camera picked up the whole thing."

"Suicide attempt?"

"Nah, don't think so. That's the weird thing. It's something else—don't ask me. I ain't a shrink."

"What'd he use?"

I stared at the shoulder. The entry wound was in the front surrounded by powder burns and large hematomas (blood bruises). It looked like a small-caliber, low-velocity bullet. It should have resulted in a puncture wound, but the nearby tissue was shredded. Hollow point?

"Cops found a .25 caliber."

A pocket or purse gun, easily concealed.

"Soon as we get him stabilized we'll do an arthrogram. I have a hunch there's some nerve damage. There's no exit wound."

He was right. The x-rays showed the small bullet, definitely a hollow-point, still lodged inside. Designed to bring down large game animals, the projectile contained a hollowed-out shape at its point, which caused it to deform rapidly once inside its target—it was designed to cause maximum damage.

The bullet was too near the main nerve cable of the shoulder, the brachial plexus, to remove safely at this point. All the surgical team could do was patch things up and see how much harm had been done.

They cleaned Justin's wound and bandaged it. The orderly was preparing to wheel him out of the ER, when his morphine-clouded eyes opened.

"Hey ... Doc ... thanks ... for ... com..."

The morphine put him out again.

"No sense hanging around, Galen," Jake said. "We'll know better in a couple of hours. I'll call you."

I nodded and turned away.

"Oh, hey, Galen."

"Yeah, Jake?"

"Funny thing. The kid didn't ask for his parents. He wanted you here."

I returned home around 5 a.m., normally the time for my early morning walk, but I had already exercised enough with the hospital visit. So I lay down, alone. Cathy had been taken from me two years before. I no longer could hear her comforting, "Wanna tell me about it?"

I closed my eyes and dozed off.

"Galen, GS, incoming."

In my slumber I returned to my days as a senior med student doing an elective in the surgical ER. My resident was one helluva doctor, and even though he worked my rump off, he was a teaching machine.

I washed the sweat off my face, sterilized my hands, and gloved up. Gunshot wounds are messy.

Very soon we heard the siren and the ambulance screeching to a halt in the turnaround. Doors slammed, and the techs rushed the cart in. The sheets covering the patient were solidly saturated with blood.

The nurses huddled around the resident, who pulled the sheet back. Everything was blood. A hole the size of my fist took the place of what should have been the woman's left breast.

Then I saw the victim's face, and a bolt of stomach acid shot up my esophagus.

"God, no! It's Carol!"

I almost threw up before turning away.

She was past any help. A .45 caliber bullet to the chest directly over the heart at close range doesn't leave much to work with.

The resident approached and sat me down.

"You knew her?"

"A classmate."

In freshman year Carol was the nervous girl at our anatomy table. I remembered hearing her unique, musical laugh.

What the hell had happened?

June, Connie, and Peggy told me and Dave later.

Carol had arrived home that evening to find her husband entangled with another woman in their bed. It wasn't the first time. She took his revolver from the bedroom dresser drawer and aimed it at the couple, then she turned it around, placed it against her breast, smiled—and pulled the trigger.

I awoke. It was 6:30 a.m.

My schedule was full that day, so I didn't have time to think. That was good.

My last patient left at 7 that evening.

I drove to the hospital and climbed the stairs to the surgical-recovery suite. As usual, it was full.

Justin lay propped up in his bed, head turned to the left, staring at the wall.

"Wouldn't it have been easier to go bungee jumping?"

His head turned toward me, and his pain-med-dulled eyes tried to focus.

"I can't ... move ... my ... right ... arm ... Doc."

I pulled over a chair and sat down.

"Feel like talking?"

"No."

"Your parents here?"

"No."

"You want me to call them?"

He shook his head.

"Okay, let me check your chart. I'll be right back. Don't go away."

That one actually got half a smile.

The surgery notes said it all: severe nerve and muscle damage. Justin wouldn't be able to use his right hand. Maybe, just maybe, later on he could undergo a procedure that would relocate muscle tendons to replace the damaged ones. That might give him some return of function.

I returned to his bedside and sat down again.

He watched me, looking for clues.

"Sure you don't wanna talk about it?"

"I wasn't trying to kill myself, Doc."

The pain meds had begun to wear off. I could see him wincing, and his speech was clearer now.

"Well, are you taking a skeet-shooting course?"

"Jesus, Doc, don't you get it?"

Suddenly it hit me. I saw the marks on his good arm and forearm. No, not needle marks like the druggies have. These were cuttings. Justin's shooting was an extreme form of cutting.

"Justin, why do you think you have a karmic debt?"

His eyes widened.

"You do understand!"

Then the floodgates opened. Justin told me about his parents, how his father had divorced his mother and left her and the children semi-destitute. The young boy faced taunts from classmates because of his small stature and his mother's lack of money. Sometimes he heard her crying and, to his child's mind, it could only be because he was to blame for his father leaving.

He remained a short, thin kid through middle school—so thin that his teachers often suspected he was being abused at home. When he attempted to bulk up by going to the local gym, his self-improvement efforts led to his being raped by one of the gym's male employees.

Eventually he reached the conclusion that he was responsible for what had happened to him. In his mind, everything bad was his fault.

"Doc, I thought about it a lot. Still do. That day I sat on a bench near the school parking lot. Can you believe it? I talked to myself. I actually had an effing conversation—me to me."

"What did you say to yourself?"

He stared at me, decided I wasn't making fun of him, cleared his throat, and reenacted the scene.

"It's go time. Has been for a while, I s'pose."

You sure as hell got that right, big guy.

"Yeah, no shit. You ever wonder how we got this far? I can't even tell you how many times I've begged God to smack the crap out of me. Seriously, it's a great way to feel amped."

I looked at the young man who saw himself a despicable, ugly little boy instead of the six-foot-tall, brilliant Adonis he had grown into. Edward Arlington Robinson's poem, "Richard Cory" crossed my mind.

So on we worked, and waited for the light,
And went without the meat, and cursed the bread;
And Richard Cory, one calm summer night,
Went home and put a bullet through his head.

No, that wasn't right. This was not depression. This was, to Justin's mind, karmic payback, retribution against that bad little boy who had caused so much trouble. Why else would he have been raped at the dawn of his manhood?

"You wanna hear more, Doc?"

"Yes."

Again he stared at me, daring me to display disdain, daring me to make fun of him. He took another breath and continued the dialogue with himself.

"God doesn't care what I do when I'm alive. He cares who I am when I die."

Well, hah, hah, hah! I guess we know why we're here. There isn't a soul alive who can make you pay for what you've done. And since you can't fix it, God doesn't care, and no one else except for me would dare risk their soul to expunge your record, this is the option. We've been over this.

"I know it. I do. But what if … what if it kills me? Can't we do it in my hand? What about my foot? Why can't I just apologize? Why can't I just tell people I'm sorry? They'll forgive me."

You've been so wayward for so long, apologies aren't enough.

"But I don't want to die. I love this life. Please, I don't want to die! Please! Please!"

Stop your whining! If I wanted you to die, I'd pump one into your brain. The shoulder's perfect. Nothing too significant's in there, as long as I avoid the artery. So let's place the shot . . . here. You dig?

He pointed right at where the bullet had entered.

"We're really doing this, aren't we?"

Yessiree, I'm serious as sin.

He turned to me.

"Doc, it took me about five minutes more, me talking to me. Then I took the gun out of my pocket, removed the clip, checked the action, and otherwise inspected my equalizer: Beretta Tomcat .25 caliber pistol. Like holding a god right in my hand!"

His lips trembled. He shrugged his good shoulder and sucked his breath in.

"I deliberately pulled back the slide. Few men will ever know how heavy a gun can seem, when you know with one-hundred-percent certainty that the next time you pull the trigger you will hit your target.

"It made a ghastly KACHENK! when it rammed the round halfway home. I figured to shoot him/me at point blank range. It would decrease the probability of hitting something vital.

"Jesus, Mother Mary, I was wrong—very, very wrong—about the vitality of the shoulder. My hand did not shake, my resolve did not quiver. I summed up all of my disgust for his/my karmic debt, and I pulled the trigger."

I tried to stop him.

"Justin, you don't need to continue this."

"Dammit, Doc, lemme finish! Or do you want me to say twelve Hail Marys and an Act of Contrition instead?"

"It's your call."

"Okay, Doc, we're at the finish line anyway. Yours truly pulled the trigger and shot himself. Justice was served on the head of a copper round last night."

He stared at me once again.

"Justin, when you get out of here, we're going to keep on talking. Okay? I'll come by every day, until Dr. Turner thinks you can go home."

"My parents have me lined up with a shrink, Doc."

"Did they visit you?"

"Yeah, my mom and stepdad were here this afternoon."

"And...?"

"They're ... uh ... really pissed at me."

He turned and stared at the wall.

"Guess that's the way it always is—seems I'm just trouble."

"The shrink is a good idea, Jus, but that doesn't mean we can't talk."

His good hand reached out to me, and I grasped it briefly before turning to leave.

I noticed the clock in the hall: 9:30 p.m.

"Hey, Bob, got a second?"

"Hey, Macario, what can I do for you?"

Macario Ghirardelli was one of the finest adolescent- and young-adult psychiatrists on the staff.

"I'm the guy that kid's parents called in. I heard what you said about us shrinks. Thanks for the good word!"

"No problem. You do indeed do good work."

"So do you."

"How much did you hear?'

"I ... uh ... was just sticking my head in and..."

"You heard it all?"

"Yeah, and what you said to him was right on target. Cutting is very common among teenagers, especially girls. They slice and scar themselves with sharp objects such as needles, razorblades, you name it. It's a defective-yet-necessary coping mechanism for anxiety and tension that comes from traumatic emotional and physical experience. It becomes self-punishing, because the teen perceives himself, or herself, as both victim and perpetrator—cause and effect. Bad things happen, because they are bad."

"Geez, Macario, I thought I was the only one with logorrhea!"

"To paraphrase the great Al Jolson, you ain't heard nuthin' yet. In Justin's case, he sees himself as the cause of his mother's divorce, their ensuing poverty status, and—the final straw—his rape at the hands of a pedophile.

"In my opinion it's a variant of post-traumatic stress disorder, so often seen in battlefield soldiers. Rape is also a common factor. So this young man was in agony, physically as well as emotionally."

"Okay, Macario. The kid's in good hands. If I can help in any way, let me know."

"Thanks, Bob. Do just what you told him you'd do: listen to him. He trusts you."

I headed toward the stairway.

As I drove home through an unexpected rainstorm, an overwhelming emotional fatigue hit me. My clothes had gotten soaked, when I ran the short distance from my parking lot to the side door. So when I got home I shucked them, changed into pajamas, and hit the mattress. I didn't feel like doing anything else.

My bed held only me. I stared at the opposite wall. Leni's stuffed toy dog and Cathy's hand-knitted scarf lay on the shelf over the little desk Cathy had given me the year before she...

Maybe I also had a karmic debt to pay.

I started talking to them, just as I once did, when they were near, and I needed to vent my thoughts and feelings about the happenings of the day. I told them about Justin—and as usual the tears came.

Cathy, Leni, is Justin right? Did I lose you both because of something I did?

I turned off the lights and lay on my side looking at the alarm clock.

It read 11:30.

Four weeks later Justin, wearing a special arm sling, was being fitted for an extender brace that kept the fingers on his right hand from becoming permanently curved into his palm. He still had no feeling or movement in that hand.

I worried about a condition called sympathetic dystrophy, when he told me about the burning-pain sensation he had begun to experience in his right arm. Sometimes a part of the nervous system goes haywire when an injury occurs. It causes pain that is very difficult to treat, a sensation that sufferers have described as burning that pierces the skin.

Fortunately, in Justin's case, it was short-lived.

He underwent intense physical therapy. It restored some shoulder movement, but the forearm and hand remained useless.

"I saw the shrink today, Doc."

"What did he say?"

"Told me I was nuts."

"Are you?"

The question seemed to startle him.

"What do you think, Doc?"

His eyes bored into me.

"You're saner than a helluva lot of people I know, Jus. Your only problem is that eight-hundred-pound guilt monkey you carry on your back."

"Mine's different, Doc."

"How so?"

"Mine's an orangutan, not a monkey."

Amazing he could joke about it. On one level he knew he didn't need to ride the guilt horse. But deeper down, the guilt had lodged where his limbic beast lurked, and it still weighed on him.

Another four months and Justin's orthopedic surgeon asked me for presurgical, medical clearance. He wanted to try a muscle/tendon transfer to restore movement to the young man's right forearm and hand.

"Do you want to do this, Justin?"

"Yeah, I'm tired of using my right hand as a hammer."

The surgery went well. Three more months and Justin held up his hand. As I watched, he opened and closed his fingers. He had become fanatical in following an exercise program to increase strength in the damaged extremity.

We continued our talks. He would stop by several times a week and shoot the breeze about school, friends, parents, and career goals. He also saw the psychiatrist weekly, but he refused to take the pills prescribed for him.

"Doc, I don't need them. I'm not crazy, I'm not depressed. I don't want to be any more of a zombie than I already am."

He had a point. I knew the psychiatrist was only trying to help him by leveling off his guilt moods with medication. But sometimes pills aren't the answer.

Besides, he had hated zombies ever since he accidently locked himself in a closet as a kid. It had scared the bejesus out of him.

"Ow! That damned bullet hurts!"

True to the trauma surgeon's prediction, Justin's bullet had started to migrate, as the muscles in his shoulder and back contracted and relaxed over time. Now it rested just inside his back near his scapula, aka wing bone.

I ran my hands over the area on his back. I could feel it.

"Think you've punished yourself enough, Jus?"

He nodded.

The surgeon asked me for another clearance before Justin's surgery.

It seemed a simple procedure to me—one often performed on the battlefield to get soldiers back in the line. But that little bullet had migrated to a spot just over the young man's lung. It had to be removed under general anesthesia with careful monitoring, just in case the procedure caused the lung to collapse.

I finished filling out the paperwork and handed it to Justin.

"Doc, could I ask you a favor?"

"Name it."

"Will you be in the operating room with me?"

"Sure."

Now it was nine months to the day, and Justin had asked the surgeon to remove the bullet on that anniversary.

I rode with him and his mother at 5 a.m. to the outpatient-surgery center. I walked behind him, as he strode determinedly to the pre-op holding area. I sat quietly, as the unit nurse told him to strip and put on a gown.

"Doc, this damned thing doesn't even cover my ass."

"So maybe the nurse is hot for you."

For a brief moment the tension left him. He laughed and changed into the gown, opened the curtain, and stuck his rump out to moon the floor staff. Then he lay back on the gurney cart, pulled a sheet over his head, and waited for the next visitor.

That was the pre-op nurse, and she started when the sheet-covered body slowly rose from the cart.

"Okay, young man, let me see your left arm."

He held it out, and she rubbed the top of his hand, waiting for a vein to pop up from the tourniquet she had wrapped around his wrist. Then she inserted the intracath needle into the vein, removed the metal insert, and capped the hub after drawing a blood sample through it. The plastic tube in his vein had been coated with a chemical to prevent clotting. Then she taped it down, so it wouldn't slip out.

"Damn, that hurt, lady!"

"I would've guessed you were a big boy," she replied.

"Yeah, wanna see it?"

"Pay no attention," I said. "He's really wound up."

She nodded, smiled back at him, and left.

The parade continued. Next the anesthesiologist arrived and reviewed Justin's medical history and drug sensitivities.

"Justin, I'm going to give you something now to relax you. It's called midazolam."

He took the vial from his pocket, drew up a dose, and stuck the syringe needle into the rubber port on the side of the intracath.

I could see Justin's facial muscles relax, as the chemical flowed through his bloodstream. He was still awake but, as he said later, he wouldn't have cared if the ceiling had fallen on him.

As the anesthesiologist headed for the door, I told him I would be accompanying Justin into the OR. I would need to change into full scrubs, so I asked him to wait five minutes. He agreed.

I headed to the surgeons' locker room, where I grabbed scrubs that I thought would fit a bear, and started to change. One of the residents recognized me.

"Hey, Galen, finally decided to become a real doctor?"

"Nah, I'm opening a butcher shop, and I want to study your techniques."

I put on the shoe covers and head cap and hurried out the door.

I walked that green mile beside the cart, as the attendant wheeled my sedated patient down the hallway to the OR. Before he slipped into unconsciousness, Justin had asked me to hold his left hand, and I did so. It seemed to take away those jitters that even the sedative could not suppress.

The OR nurse helped me into sterile gown and gloves and put the mask around my face. I took my place at the operating table on Justin's left side. He looked up at me and tried to talk, but the drug had dried his mouth. I patted his arm, and he smiled. I had seen it many times on many patients.

It was a little boy's smile.

The anesthesiologist hooked up an IV to the tube in Justin's arm and nodded at me.

Now it would begin.

He placed an oxygen mask over the patient's face and an oxygen sensor on his left second finger then told him to take some big breaths. As Justin inhaled, I saw the other doctor push down on syringe plungers containing knock-out drugs and muscle paralyzers.

Within seconds Justin's eyelids fluttered then closed half-way. His jaw dropped, and his chest stopped its normal breathing motion.

The anesthesiologist pulled his jaw down even farther, stuck the laryngoscope down his throat, and quickly inserted a tube into his windpipe. Then he connected the tube to a machine that would do Justin's breathing for him.

The scrub nurse taped the tube in place, applied lubricating ointment to Justin's half-open but unconscious eyes, and taped his eyelids shut.

"He's under."

The OR attendants rolled the unconscious patient onto his left side and strapped him into position. They extended his right arm above his head to give a better view of the bullet site on his shoulder.

I moved to the other side and stood behind the surgical assistant, who performed the multiple skin cleanings and preparation. Then the surgeon moved forward and the instrument litany began.

"Scalpel."

He made a three-inch incision into the skin and fat. Blood oozed out, and the assistant used the electrical cautery to seal the leaking small blood vessels.

"We got a pumper! Clamp!"

The incision had nicked a tiny artery. It was spurting. The surgeon clamped it and tied it off.

"Retractor."

He placed a small gadget that looks like two forks bent sideways in the wound and expanded it to spread the muscle fibers apart.

"Thar she be! 'Tis Moby Dick, the great white whale!"

"I didn't know surgeons could read, Tom," I muttered.

He chuckled softly and called for the bullet extractor. He grabbed the dark-gray ball of metal and gently wiggled it out. I could see the lung lining, the pleura, glistening at the bottom of the bullet hole.

The surgeon waved the bullet extractor in triumph.

"No doubt now, Galen. Your patient is the proud father of a baby, hollow-point .25."

The nurse held out a glass specimen jar filled with preservative fluid, and the surgeon dropped the bullet into its bassinet. I heard the clink when it hit bottom.

"Okay, Sam, irrigate and close. He'll need a drain left in for a few days."

The wound would fill with body fluids and blood and not heal properly, unless the stuff could easily drain out.

The assistant inserted the rubber drain after carefully flushing out the wound three times. He checked for any remaining bullet fragments then closed the opening in layers from the deepest on out.

I walked around to the other side and watched Justin lying there in that chemical state somewhere between sleep and death. Technically and legally he was an adult, but in reality he was a child, a helpless and emotionally bruised child.

Why did this happen to him?

"You guys finished?" the anesthesiologist asked.

"Yeah, go ahead, bring him up," the surgeon responded.

The nurse and attendant rolled Justin onto his back and removed the straps.

The anesthesiologist turned to me.

"Your patient isn't going to like what comes next."

Yeah, I knew that. The doctor would stop the drugs that kept Justin's muscles paralyzed. Then he would administer the reversal drugs—chemicals that counteracted the medications that had rendered the patient unconscious.

At just the right moment, after removing the tape from his eyelids and face, the anesthesiologist would yank the breathing tube out of Justin's windpipe. When that happened, the slowly awakening patient usually tried to sit up and cough his head off.

That's exactly what happened. Justin's eyelids fluttered then opened. The anesthesiologist yanked out the tube, and Justin tried to sit bolt upright, coughing and squeaking out a hoarse "shit!"

As they wheeled him out to the recovery room, I turned and looked once more at the bottle containing the bullet.

He opened his eyes. The drugs weren't quite out of him yet.

"Is ... it... out?"

"Yep. One helluva big orangutan, boy."

He smiled and quickly fell asleep.

I walked to the waiting room, where his mother had been dozing. When I cleared my throat, she woke up, startled.

"Is he ... is he all right?"

"Just fine. He's in recovery now. I'll go back in and check on him in a few minutes."

"Thank God!"

"Tough time, huh?"

"You don't know the half of it, Doctor."

She told me about her life and the difficulties both she and Justin had experienced, after her first husband deserted them. It was straight out of a soap opera.

By the time she was done, all I could do was shake my head. And I thought I had been through the wringer!

I returned to the recovery room. Justin was awake.

"Ready to pee, kid?"

"Wh … wha…?"

His voice was still hoarse from the breathing tube.

"When you can pee and hold down some fluids we can take you home. Wanna give it a try, big fella?"

He nodded, and I waved the recovery-room nurse over.

"Let's try him out."

She pulled the curtains closed around his cart and handed him a plastic male urinal.

"What am I supposed to do with that?"

He coughed to clear his throat.

"Guess."

He actually blushed.

I tossed it in his lap and stepped outside the curtain. I could hear him succeeding. When he finished I poked my head back in.

"Here. Hope it tastes good, Doc."

"Good boy. Now, hold down the apple juice and you've made it to third base."

He sucked on the straw stuck in the juice container then belched.

"How do I get to home plate, Doc?"

"First, don't throw up. Second, try sitting on the edge of the bed. I'll stand beside you. Third, if you make it that far, get out of your beautiful designer hospital gown and put your clothes on. I'll help you with that."

"Tired of seeing me naked, Doc?"

"Justin, I've been doing this longer than your mama's been alive. There's only two basic body models, and I've seen more than my share of both of them."

Justin was still not quite with it, but he smiled when his mother rushed up and hugged him. He winced and let out an "ow," when her hand pressed on his back.

An hour later and changed back into my civvies, I walked beside the wheelchair, as the attendant pushed it out to the waiting area.

Back home and sitting on the edge of the bed in my pajamas I spoke again to my beloved ghosts. It ended when I broke down and cried. I couldn't shake off my demons as easily as Justin had.

At 11 p.m. I lay back on the bed, my mind wanting to scream.

Leni, Cathy, why couldn't I have saved you? It was all my fault.

I waited for an answer, knowing all the while there would be none. Finally I fell asleep.

The phone rang. The clock dial read 4:06.

"Doc, hey, Doc?"

"Yes, Chet. What's up?"

"Doc, it's a boy!"

No Deposit, No Return

Have you noticed that no matter who we elect, he is just as bad as the one he replaces?

—Will Rogers

"Politicians!"

My colleague and friend from residency stared at his iced tea. He was not a happy camper.

"So, what else is new, Dave?"

"Maybe it's just me, Bob. Maybe I'm getting old."

Dave Abbot looked up from his drink. Unlike me, he had kept in decent shape over the years since our post-graduate medical training. He was still the lean, well-dressed, ex-Navy doc I had met over four decades earlier. He did not look the three-score-plus that he was.

The noise in the hospital cafeteria rose briefly then quieted down.

"Dave, I agree. Unlike me, you're getting older. So what's the problem?"

"I just had a woman in my office the other day. Congressman's wife. Smart, good looking, great personality. Guess why she came in?"

A no-brainer.

"Let's see. Her pol husband has strayed and taken up with some chippie legislative aide or assistant from the congressional secretarial pool. Now he's gonna dump her. Right?"

His eyes widened.

"How'd you know?"

Dave had been happily married to his childhood sweetheart for over forty years. He considered even looking at another woman out of bounds.

"Human nature. Power does something to people. Pretty soon they become solipsistic and..."

"Whoa, bear breath. You're doing it again."

"Eh?"

"That big-word stuff."

"Okay, okay, Dr. Abbot, how's this? When politicians start to believe their own PR crap, they think the sun, moon, and stars revolve around them. *Capite, paisan?*"

"Yeah."

I stared out at the nurses, orderlies, and other hospital personnel milling about the food lines. Random memories of my Leni and Cathy, who had each once sat across from me in that very room, separated only by a few years, made my mind wander momentarily.

"You okay, Bob?"

I snapped out of my reverie.

"Do you know how lucky you are, my friend?"

"Huh?"

"You have your wife, kids, grandkids—sometimes I wonder what it would have been like if..."

He saw the look on my face. He knew my personal history.

"Uh ... Bob, you were gonna tell me how you guessed about my patient."

"Okay, okay. Did I ever tell you about the No Deposit, No Return Club?"

We each took a sip of tea. He looked at me expectantly. I shifted my black bag off the table onto a side chair and leaned back.

"It started about twenty-five years ago..."

"Tony, there's a woman at the door. She seems pretty upset."

My Cathy, as did my Leni, always called me by my middle name. She had rubbed my arm gently, until I awoke. I had decided to sleep late that Sunday. I had no hospital patients that needed my attention, and Saturday had been riotously busy.

I was tired.

Cathy, dear Cathy, had gotten up at her usual time and promised to fix me a special Sunday brunch. When she told me, I mumbled something about her being "good enough to eat" then quickly fell back asleep.

That lasted maybe five seconds. I awoke to her pushing on my chest and talking loudly.

"Tony, wake up. This poor woman is really upset."

I didn't shave. It was only Cathy standing in the bedroom doorway that prevented me from walking into my office in my pajamas. I dressed. By the time I did meet the woman I was fully awake—yet another med-school legacy.

She sat in the lounge chair, twisting and turning the white handkerchief she held tightly, her facial makeup streaked from crying. Tear-puffed, hazel eyes centered a rounded face bracketed by uncombed, light-brown hair.

"Sorry to keep you waiting. What seems to be the problem, Mrs. ..."

"I ... I ... I'm Ethel Saltzman. I..."

Tears overcame her.

Cathy had joined me. She moved to the woman's side and calmly touched her shoulder.

"Ethel, let me take you to the ladies' room."

She turned to me and shook her head, as she led the woman away.

About ten minutes later, a rejuvenated Ethel Saltzman stepped into my examining room. She attempted a weak smile and sat down.

"How did you find us, Mrs. Saltzman?"

"One of my friends comes to you. She said you're here all the time."

Cathy covered her mouth to keep from laughing. We had just had a discussion about that very topic the previous day. She wanted me to take more time off.

Looking back, I wish I had.

I miss you, Cathy.

"How may I help you, Mrs. Saltzman?"

"Do you know my husband, Doctor?"

A light bulb went on.

"Norman 'Salty' Saltzman. Senator Saltzman?"

"Yes, he's my husband."

I remained silent.

"He … he told me this morning … he's going to leave me. He wants a divorce."

Cathy interjected.

"Have there been … problems?"

"Not that I knew about, Mrs. Galen. We've been married twenty years. I met Norman when he first ran for Congress. I worked on his campaign. Then, when he decided to try for the Senate, I ran his strategy committee for him."

I was curious.

"Mrs. Saltzman, when do you think things changed between the two of you?"

She froze for a moment, as though the thought was new to her.

"You know, it seemed to start after I had foot surgery."

Cathy and I shot quizzical glances at each other.

"Uh … Norman sometimes gets a little aggressive when we … uh … you know … and he likes to nibble on my toes. He seems to need it to be able to…"

It was a bit more than I needed to hear, but I have to admit it was fascinating from a psycho-pathology perspective.

So, Salty Saltzman had a foot fetish.

They're called paraphilias. For some folks, becoming intimate involves an attachment with a different part of the body than the usual ones. In Salty's case, it was the female foot that turned him on.

Podophiliacs, as they're called, come in several flavors: Some like big feet, others prefer small. Some fixate on slight differences in the shape of toes—turning them either on or off. When Ethel needed foot surgery, the bloom had dropped off the rose for Norman.

Cathy sat quietly, as I explained what had happened. Mrs. Saltzman seemed to gain hope then broke down again.

"Maybe I can get the podiatrist to restore my foot to what it was," she said between sobs.

No doubt about it, Ethel was desperate.

"I'm not sure that's going to work, Mrs. Saltzman. Fetishists have very specific … uh … tastes when it comes to their particular object of desire."

We finished our discussion, and Ethel's face took on a surprisingly relaxed expression. I have seen that same facial expression in those who finally decide to commit suicide.

"I'm going to tell my friends about you. Is that okay?"

I nodded. What else could I do? Cathy had put her arm around my waist.

Ethel Saltzman underwent her foot surgery two weeks later, and Norman divorced her two months after that.

Ethel became a regular patient, and as time passed more and more discarded politicians' wives visited the office. It got to the point where I joked to one of them that they were like no-deposit, no-return bottles.

Then one day I received an engraved invitation to speak at one of the ex-wives' gatherings.

I'm not big on such things, but Cathy insisted, so I agreed. I wrote a brief talk about self-worth, hoping that no one would ask to hear it.

We showed up at the nearby Italian café and saw the entire back dining room occupied by our patients. They were all attractive, intelligent women, but all had been discarded by idiots—men who didn't realize how lucky they had been.

I glanced at each one and mentally ticked off the personality traits of her foolish ex-husband: narcissist, sociopath, alcoholic, podophile, pedophile, wife abuser, male menopause (andropause), bisexual, and more.

Ethel Saltzman saw us arrive and walked over.

"Dr. Galen, Mrs. Galen, I just thought I'd let you know. Remember Norman?"

We nodded.

"He lost his re-election. Guess what he came down with?"

We waited for the punch line.

She smiled.

"Hoof-and-mouth disease."

Cathy and I burst out laughing.

"Come on, you two, let me introduce you to the crowd. I think some of our members haven't met you yet."

We walked into the back dining room and were greeted with polite applause.

"Ladies, most of you know our guests, but I'm going to introduce them anyway. Please welcome Dr. Robert and Mrs. Cathy Galen."

More polite applause, then we heard a voice from the audience.

"Mrs. Galen, Cathy, how did you and the doctor meet?"

My Cathy, my wonderful Cathy, started to laugh.

"The big oaf knocked me off my feet."

I had to defend myself.

"She's right, ladies, I did knock her off her feet—literally. I wasn't watching where I was going in the hospital corridor and knocked her flat on her keister."

Cathy looked at me, winked, and put her arms around me. Then she kissed me in front of everyone.

"He's just a big teddy bear, folks," she said, laughing.

The applause subsided, as Ethel Saltzman stepped over to an easel covered by a drape.

"Dr. Galen, Mrs. Galen, we welcome you to our little gathering.

She reached over and, with a flourish, pulled the drape away from a large placard. The women in the group stood up and erupted into cheers and whistles.

The sign read: NO DEPOSIT, NO RETURN CLUB

Things Aren't Always What They Seem

"Dr. Galen, take a look out the window."

Barbara pointed at the glass sliding door. Out in the parking lot a large limo had pulled in, and a liveried attendant stepped out. He walked carefully to the rear passenger door, opened it, and waited, as a well-dressed woman gracefully stepped out. The chauffeur took her hand and escorted her to my door then backed away.

"Are you Dr. Galen?"

A husky voice redolent of a long-dead movie star caressed the air.

"Yes, ma'am."

"I would like a brief checkup."

"Certainly. Please come in."

I led the new patient to the first examining room. I waited, until she sat down, then I took a chair, my pen poised over the data-entry sheet. She chuckled softly, as she looked at my Goodwill couture. The clothes she wore would easily have consumed several months of my income. She casually waved a wrist adorned with a diamond-and-imperial-jade bracelet.

"My name is Lavinia, Lavinia Portenté."

She waited expectantly, but I didn't know who the hell she was.

"Yes, Ms. Portenté?"

She seemed disappointed, but she politely gave me her address, date of birth, and medical history—and she asserted that there was nothing significant of that nature in her past.

I asked her to put on an exam gown then left the room, telling her to call out when ready.

Several minutes later I heard, "All right, Dr. Galen."

I began my examination at the top and worked my way down: nothing unusual, except for an Adam's apple on her throat—and, of course, the moment of truth.

I finished up and stepped out once more to allow my patient to dress.

I reentered the examining room after hearing, "I'm dressed, Doctor." I detailed my findings and recommended some lab tests.

Portenté agreed, smiled, and stepped out to the secretary's desk. Shortly afterwards, Barbara walked into my office and said, "Well?"

"Fascinating patient, eh?" I replied.

"And…?"

I showed her my best poker face.

She waited.

"And…?"

Barbara didn't give up easily.

"That was Louis Porter. He does quite a good imitation of Marlene Dietrich, doesn't he?"

Yasmin's Song

Oh, why do we allow these people
To breed back to the monkey's nest,
To increase our country's burdens
When we should only breed the best?
Oh, you wise men take up the burden,
And make this you(r) loudest creed,
Sterilize the misfits promptly—
All are not fit to breed!
Then our race will be strengthened and bettered,
And our men and our women be blest,
Not apish, repulsive and foolish,
For the best will breed the best.

—Dr. William de Jarnette, director,
Western State Hospital, Staunton, Virginia, 1938

"Trick or treat!"

They stood at my front door—witches, goblins, skeletons, devils, lawyers, politicians and IRS agents—all pint-sized versions of adult nightmares.

Cathy nudged me.

"Give them the candy, Tony!"

Tony was her special name for me. After all, I was born Roberto Antonio Galen.

I obeyed, throwing candy, as well as pennies, nickels, and dimes, into the outstretched paper bags. I watched little eyes light up behind their masks and a few—just a few—even managed "thanks, Mister" and "Happy Halloween," before running back down the walk to extort more goodies from the next house.

Cathy smiled at my perplexed face.

"Tony, didn't you ever go trick-or-treating?"

My beloved second wife already knew the answer, but sometimes she liked to tease me. My whole life had been a trick or treat, with emphasis on "trick."

How I enjoyed her teasing. It often led to more … uh … pleasurable activities.

"Why celebrate ghosts and goblins? Aren't I devil enough for you?"

I twirled an imaginary handlebar mustache.

She put her arms around me and whispered, "Trick or treat!"

Then came the phone call.

Certain activities should not be interrupted, but I sighed and grabbed Mr. Bell's damned invention to stop its incessant ringing.

"Doctor Galen?"

I snarled out a "yes."

"Dr. Galen, do you have late hours?"

I stared at the wall clock in front of me: 9 p.m.

"What's the problem?"

"Uh … we've never been to see you before, but our little girl is running a fever of 104 and holding her ears and screaming. We don't want to expose her to an emergency room."

"Bring her over now."

I heaved a sigh and hung up.

"See, you really do have a soft spot, Tony."

Cathy massaged my clenched jaw.

No, I don't, but this was the job I signed on for, when I took the Hippocratic Oath. People, especially kids, don't get sick just on weekdays.

She put a finger on my nose and pulled on my ear.

That always worked.

"I'm no Mother Teresa, young lady. You know how much I enjoy an uninterrupted evening reading and listening to music and discussing Plato with you."

"And canoodling?"

She had a way of batting those long eyelashes.

I didn't have to reply. Cathy knew me all too well. She also knew that when my mental hibernation was disrupted, I would quickly become my eponym: the bear.

"Need any help?"

"Nah, you stay here. I shall return!"

"Aye-aye, General MacArthur!"

I turned on the office lights and waited. My mind brought forth scathing comments about parents waiting until nighttime before seeking help for sick kids.

I heard the car pull in the parking lot and went to open the door, when the outside light illuminated not only the patient but my brain.

Mother and father walked slowly up the path, each holding an arm of a crying young girl between them. In the half-shadow I saw something else.

"Dr. Galen?"

"Yes, come in. I'm sorry I didn't get your name on the phone."

"Lon Thomas. This is my wife, Nabila. And this is Yasmin. Say hello to the doctor, Yas."

A tremulous, hoarse "hello" greeted me.

Lon Thomas was a mutt.

Remember Frankie Fontaine as "Crazy" Guggenheim on the old "Jackie Gleason Show?"

That was Lon. At six-feet-two and two-hundred-eighty pounds, he resembled a cross between a Shar-Pei and a Bulldog. But when he opened his mouth, it was baritone honey.

Far from being a mutt, Nabila Thomas was the Estonian Nefertiti: stylish dress, eyes taking in everything and making instant assessments.

Speaking of old TV shows, if you remember "Rocky and Bullwinkle," you will instantly know what I mean when I say that her voice was identical to Natasha Badenov.

"Yasmin, dear, come. Sit on the table and let the doctor look at you."

I gazed at the young girl wiping tears from her face, and I knew.

Yasmin Thomas was ten going on eleven. She couldn't have been more than three-feet-six at the time. Her short forearms attached to small, stubby-fingered hands, and her almond-shaped eyes and small ears were set in a face broader than usual for a child of her age.

I took her hands and held them, trying to put her at ease by smiling. It also gave me a chance to look at her palms. Yes, only one skin crease.

Lon and Nabila Thomas watched me silently, as I addressed their daughter.

"Yas, I'm going to shine a light in your nose and mouth, and then we'll look at your ears. Is that okay with you?"

Eyes devoid of even childhood guile looked at me. Slowly her head nodded, and she returned my smile.

I turned on my scope light and held it out to her. She took it and handed it back to me.

"Open wide now."

A thick, fissured tongue protruded from a square-jawed face perched on a shortened neck.

"Now let's take a look at your nose."

I put a finger on her flattened nose, and she laughed. Both sides clear.

Now came the tricky part. From the way she held her head, it looked like her left ear was giving her pain. If the examination made the pain worse, the game was over.

"Yas, I'm going to look at your good ear. Let's see, I'll bet it's this one."

I pointed at her right ear, and she nodded.

I took a quick look. Canal and drum were fine.

"Now, Yas, I'm going to need your help. I have to look at the ear that hurts you. I'll be as quick as I can, but if it hurts, you tell me."

This time I didn't pull back on her ear. I directed my scope light into the canal and saw the characteristic signs of a pretty bad infection. Fortunately the ear drum hadn't ruptured yet.

Those puppy-dog brown eyes kept looking right at me, as I sat down and faced her parents.

"Yasmin has a bad middle-ear infection. She gets a lot of them, doesn't she?"

Both parents nodded.

"Did you know about her condition before she was born?"

Nabila got right to the point.

"Why do you ask, Doctor?"

Then Lon got there as well.

"Did we do something *wrong*?"

I could see the frowns on both their faces. This couple had been hurt by the stupidity of others. I shook my head.

"Yasmin is one very special and lucky little girl. I am amazed at how well-behaved and cooperative she is. It takes a remarkable couple to raise a child with Down's syndrome."

Sometimes having too much of a good thing is not good.

We walk upright and call ourselves humans, because of the presence of forty-six genetic control panels lurking inside every one of our body's cells, save two: sperm and egg. Our chromosomes contain the blueprints and operating systems that make us what we are. Damage even one of those control panels—or change it—and what results is a blessing to one or an abomination to another.

It used to be called Mongolism, because the child's facial features resulted from a replicated control panel called chromosome 21. Those who specialize in the study of chromosomes—the geneticists—call it Trisomy 21.

This genetic flip of the dice can occur in several ways. When Papa's sperm, with its twenty-three chromosomes, bursts through the defenses of Mama's ovum, also containing twenty-three chromosomes, the process allows a separate, new life to begin.

With Down's syndrome, Chromosome 21 mysteriously splits, creating an extra copy, and three in all.

Mother Nature had played that trick on Yasmin, but the Thomases had greeted her as a treat.

Yes, she had her limitations. Her voice was somewhat hoarse because of thick vocal cords. She never achieved the level of conscious deceit that other kids do, as they hit their preteens.

Like George Washington, Yasmin could not tell a lie.

I asked Nabila and Lon to tell me the story of their child's birth.

Nabila's Eastern European voice filled me in.

"Those oh-so-smart doctors said I wasn't pregnant. For three months, I tell them I am pregnant, and they say, 'No, you're not.' When they see me at six months, they say, 'Hot damn, you're pregnant!'"

"What was worse," Lon added, "when Yasmin was born, this young doctor comes in, looks at us, and asks us when we thought things had gone wrong."

"Yah, he says the word 'wrong.' Lon looks at him, and I'm afraid Lon would punch doctor. Lon is sweetheart, but don't get him angry!"

The big guy's face broke into a broad grin.

"I think the doctor stepped back, when I asked what was wrong with him. Then he says, 'Your daughter is a Mongoloid. She has Down's syndrome. We'll help you put her up for adoption.'"

I wasn't surprised. As I have learned many times, intelligence doesn't automatically convey common sense.

"What did you tell him, Mr. Thomas?"

"Call me Lon, Dr. Galen. I told him in my own inimitable way to get lost."

Nabila shook her finger at him.

"No, you told doctor to go autocopulate!"

"You've always had a way with words, my love," he replied.

We laughed. I wrote a prescription for eardrops to relieve the pain and shrink Yasmin's swollen drum. I also prescribed an antibiotic. Children with Down's syndrome are much more susceptible to bad infections of the ears.

We talked a while more, as the Thomases filled me in on their own lives.

Lon was one of those rare humans whose voice could charm Satan himself. Using his voice professionally, he had played the unseen narrator for countless radio and television commercials and programs. Tune in to The Learning Channel, the National Geographic Channel, and others, and almost certainly you'll hear his mellifluous voice.

Nabila was another *rara avis*. She was a child of the world, spending her youth in European, Middle Eastern, and southern Asian countries. A polyglot linguist, well-grounded in philosophy and political science, she served as a war correspondent and photographer who went where angels and men feared to tread.

When they left, Yasmin was humming an unidentifiable tune and happily licking a lollipop.

I was tired. It was almost 11 p.m. I headed to the residence part of my not-so-vast complex.

"I didn't hear any screaming or angry rants, Tony. What did you do wrong?"

"Mrs. Galen, let me show you what's wrong."

And I did. Then she showed me what was right.

Afterward, Cathy drifted into peaceful sleep, but my troubled mind rode a nightmare of memory.

"Hey, City Boy, ever breed animals?"

"Huh?"

"Animals, you know ... cows, pigs, chickens."

"Why? You got some illegitimate kids no one knows about?"

Dave, my medical school roommate, pushed me off the tree stump I was sitting on and tried to "wrassle me"—as folk in his part of the world called it—until I got the upper hand and pinned him down.

He was taller, but I was stronger.

It was early spring of our third year, and we had one of those rare, two-day weekends off from ward duty. Why stay in Richmond, when that quiet, rural haven was only four hours away? Besides, we were so church-mouse poor that gasoline, even at twenty-five cents a gallon, was a stretch.

So I showed Dave how we used to survive in my old neighborhood. I took him to some vacant lots—as well as some areas no sensible human would traverse—to scavenge soda and beer bottles. It didn't take long to accumulate enough in deposit returns for the couple of bucks we needed fill up the tank of his Volkswagen beetle.

Voila! Road trip.

Later, he returned the favor by demonstrating what he did with bottles. He picked up a pebble then took a gadget out of his back pocket—a whittled, Y-shaped tree branch onto which he had tied two pieces of an old tire inner tube connected to a small leather pouch.

A sling shot!

He popped that stone into the pouch, took aim, and shattered a pop bottle he had perched on the fence rail. I stopped him before he could send a poor little gray squirrel sitting peacefully in a tree to squirrel heaven.

We wrassled again. I pinned him again.

"So tell me about animal breeding, Country Boy. And don't say anything about past girlfriends, or I might tell Connie."

He pointed out across the pasture.

"See those cows, City Boy?"

"Sho 'nuff, Lum."

"Well, listen up, Abner," he replied, playing the second half of a popular radio twosome. "Cows didn't look like that when they first became cows. We humans bred 'em for the things we wanted: size, ease of feeding and calving, and more."

"I'm not sure you'd have made it past the selection process."

"Strange you should say that. Did I ever tell you about my Uncle Andrew?"

"Nope," I said, picking up a blade of grass to chew on.

"Why don't we go visit him?"

I froze for a moment.

"Please, tell me he's not a conjer man."

I was referring to Aunt Hattie, the strange old woman Dave had taken me to visit the year before—the woman who had warned me about the Bone Man.

"No, but it'll be an experience. Come on."

We dropped by the house to let Dave's mother know we'd be gone for a while, then we drove off in the VW. It took two hours, but we were still young enough to enjoy pointless driving. Dave pulled up to the gray, castle-like, multi-storied hospital and parked.

"Is your uncle sick, Dave?"

"*They* think so."

Then I realized where we were, though I had never been there before. I had heard about the place in lectures back at school. It was a state-run hospital established to treat and hold what were commonly called the most "difficult" cases.

We showed our medical-school ID badges to the guard, who passed us through a locked, iron gate into the main corridor. It was lit by naked light bulbs dangling from wires. Down the hallway we approached a large room euphemistically labeled SUN PARLOR.

We passed another guard and entered a gray-painted, cinderblock space highlighted with one small window covered by iron bars inside and out. Within its confines men and women had congregated in gray-striped, pajama-like outfits. They shuffled back and forth, leaned with their heads against the wall and, in some cases, banged those heads at rhythmic intervals.

My skin crawled. This was the therapeutic equivalent of Dachau, Buchenwald, and more.

We approached a man sitting on the floor, swaying back and forth. At first, I thought he was a child. His head was small—it didn't fit the large body beneath it. His face was like a blank sheet of paper, devoid of emotion behind eyes. He saw nothing of our world.

Dave turned to me.

"This is my Uncle Andrew."

He crouched down and spoke to the distorted creature.

The man didn't reply.

Dave turned to me as he rose.

"So how do you like my uncle, Bob?"

I looked around at the inhabitants of that room: incomplete, human jigsaw puzzles whose very appearance assaulted the eyes.

"Who are these people?"

He took hold of my arm.

"Come on, let's get outta here."

As we drove back to the farm, I listened as a side of my friend emerged—one I had never seen or heard before.

"Bob, remember when you joked that I wouldn't have made the cut in a breeding exercise?"

I nodded and tried to inject some levity by muttering "I didn't know you were a cow, Dave. All bull, yes…"

The look on his face shut me up.

"Bob, I wasn't supposed to be born. The State of Virginia had declared that my family was defective."

I stared at him for a moment.

"What are you talking about?"

My incredulity offended him.

"City Boy, you've got a lot to learn about history. Just shut up and let me talk, okay?"

"Okay."

"Andrew is my father's older brother. As you saw, somehow he wasn't right from the day he was born. Even now I can't explain what went wrong to make him like that."

He hesitated.

"You know about eugenics?"

Yes, I knew. Two decades before, the world had barely defeated a monster who sought to conquer it with his Aryan *ubermensch*. I also knew that my own family—my ethnic group, as they say today—was not really wanted in the U.S. of A., when they arrived here in 1914. The leaders back then feared our genes would pollute the superior Anglo-Saxon/Nordic stock.

Then Dave delivered his blockbuster.

"Both my parents were, by state law, supposed to be sterilized so that their so-called defects wouldn't get passed on. Virginia was in the forefront of laws passed to prevent the spread of deviance, imbecility, feeble-mindedness, perversion, and epilepsy."

"Your mother's side, too?"

"Yep, Ma has a cousin with Down's syndrome. According to the political geniuses back then, her entire family was supposed to be sterilized—neutered—so that no more generations could be produced by inferior stock. They sent Aunt Beth to the Virginia Colony for Epileptics and Feeble-Minded in Lynchburg. She was forcibly sterilized there.

"Bob, all those people you saw at the hospital have been sterilized by state mandate. And guess what? That late unlamented bastard Hitler based his ideas for a master race on the scientific papers of so-called eugenics philosophers and doctors in the United States—especially Virginia!"

I let that remark sink in.

"Look, Dave, you're here, so obviously nothing happened to your parents, right?"

He pulled the car off the road, shut off the engine, and turned to me.

"My folks hid out in the mountains until I was born. Only then was it safe to return home. The rest of my relatives went under the kni..."

He broke down into tears.

We sat in silence for awhile. Then I got out and walked around to the driver's side. He slid across to the passenger seat, and I drove the rest of the way.

I felt tired when we reached the little farmhouse. The first thing Dave did was surprise his parents with hugs. Then he headed for his room and stayed there the rest of the day.

That Sunday, I joined Dave and his family at the little Baptist church five miles down the road.

I saw faces in the congregation, faces not quite right, wrinkled by time. I wondered whether the state had improved its gene pool by neutering them.

The next week, back in Richmond, we sneaked out of a midday medical conference and walked down Broad Street to the Virginia State Library. Our med school IDs gained us entry and help from the reference librarian.

It took awhile. This was long before the days of computerized data searches, let alone Google and online research, but she knew what she was doing. Soon she presented us with a stack of documents and brittle, brown newspapers from the early 1920s.

We stretched them out before us on the long, dark-oak table.

The cold, black print contained articles about the Virginia laws we sought, including the 1924 Sterilization Act and the 1927 *Buck versus Bell* case against involuntary sterilization, where even the Chief Justice of the United States Supreme Court, Oliver Wendell Holmes, sided with the sterilization advocates.

Our eyes widened as we saw the names of prominent doctors, including some of our own professors and the man who headed the American Medical Association, all of whom supported the laws when they were enacted.

Then Dave pointed at another paper.

"You wouldn't be here, either, Bob."

I looked down at the title of the law authorized by Congress: The Immigration Restriction Act of 1924. It specifically sought to limit the entry into the United States of "dysgenic Italians and Eastern European Jews."

Although not included in the act, its advocates strongly recommended the involuntary sterilization of "ethnic defectives."

A cold chill enveloped me, and I had to sit down.

And then I awoke in a sweat, realizing that I had been dreaming part of my painful reverie.

"What's wrong, Tony?"

"N ... nothing," I stammered, "just a bad dream."

It really wasn't, but I couldn't tell her—not then. The monstrosity of what those so-called scientists and social-planning elites had done staggered me.

Beethoven, St. Paul the apostle and, irony of ironies, some of those who had supported eugenics, such as Alexander Graham Bell and Winston Churchill—and even that Austrian paper-hanger named Adolph—would not have existed had those restrictions been imposed before they were born.

Even worse was the law of unintended consequences. The mass sterilizations and human destruction of the Third Reich, even *Ha Shoah*—The Holocaust—had stemmed from the eugenics laws that originated here, in the Land of the Free.

The turning away of boatloads of Jewish refugees, and their subsequent torture and death at the hands of a psychopath, was due to the mindset of a Southern Democrat congressional coalition that persuaded President Franklin D. Roosevelt to refuse them entry—because they were "racially undesirable."

The next day I worked through a full patient load. Then, as things quieted down, Barbara called out from the waiting room.

"Dr. Galen, please pick up the phone."

"Who is it?"

"Lon Thomas."

"Dr. Galen, Nabila and I wanted you to know that Yasmin is much better ... and that we wanted to thank you ... for understanding."

Over the years the Thomas family visited me many more times, and they gave me the pleasure that can be enjoyed only by a doctor whose practice allows for following children as they grow and mature.

Yasmin Thomas grew into an amazing adult. No, she was not an Einstein, but thanks to her parents, who disregarded the shameful ignorance displayed by the medical profession when she was born, Yasmin became the unexpected treat.

When digital cameras became available, Nabila gave Yasmin a basic one and showed her how to point through the viewfinder and click the shutter.

So Yasmin would walk through crowds of people, seeing the world through those almond guileless eyes.

Point/click. Point/click.

She hummed to herself, as she captured fascinating—and unfiltered—views of people and life. Birds and insects did not fly away, as she aimed her camera's electronic memory at them. People who spent their entire lives masking their feelings from others seemed not to want to hide from the lens of that innocent mind.

The truth was Yasmin's Song.

Justice Is

"If the law supposes that," said Mr. Bumble, "the law is a ass—a idiot."

—Charles Dickens, Oliver Twist,

CHAPTER 51 (FIRST PUBLISHED 1837–1839)

"I find the defendant guilty."

I sat there in the back of the small, county courtroom. The wooden benches were uncomfortably hard, and the slightly blue-violet glow of the fluorescent lights produced a migraine-inducing flicker. Also, the air conditioning wasn't working, so the sweaty aroma of several previous trials lent an overcast atmosphere to the legal purgatory.

The judge was very sure of his verdict. Besides, he was hungry, and his hemorrhoids were acting up. He cracked jokes with the police officers now milling around the bench.

The arresting officer swaggered, posing *muy macho* in his uniform. He flashed a thumbs-up to his colleagues, another notch for his conviction record. He was batting .700, but it was professional. Not personal, not malicious.

The defense attorney shook hands with the county prosecutor and shared jokes and coffee. He would receive his fee despite the outcome.

My patient sat in the front row, quietly stunned. He kept shaking his head and whispering "no." He had just been convicted of being a "Peeping Tom."

What was the problem?

He was innocent.

Yes, I know, the prisons are filled with the innocent. But this time I held a personal stake in the matter. When my patient supposedly was peering through the ground-floor windows of some nearby townhouses, he and I were discussing computer systems on the telephone.

Brad Lester was a quiet kid. The youngest of three brothers, he was ten years old when his mother, a divorced government worker, first brought him to see me. Soft-spoken and shy, he watched his older brother go through the ritual torture of the yearly school physical.

Aaron Lester was outgoing, aggressive, athletic, a non-stop talker, who only shut up when I thumped his knees with my reflex hammer. His involuntary knee-jerks caused the younger boy to giggle at the jokes our bodies play on us.

"What's so funny, runt?"

The twelve year-old was ready to jump off the table and pound on his sibling.

"Sit down, Aaron," I growled, "I'm not done yet."

Elder bears hold amazingly persuasive powers over pre-teens.

Brad stuck out his tongue at his brother.

"Don't forget, kiddo, you're next."

His tongue quickly retracted.

It was during Aaron's vision screening that I noticed a peculiar behavior pattern in Brad. He had become quite focused. He closed his eyes and listened intently to his brother identifying the letters on the chart and the numbers inside each of the different-colored circles.

It was just a hunch, but I played it.

"Brad, since you're already in here, let me check your eyes, too. Hop up on the chair and tell me what you see."

He looked into the vision-tester and rattled off a series of numbers. It was meant to test color vision, and his response mirrored Aaron's. Then I asked him to read a line of letters and, once again, he gave the list Aaron had given.

They weren't correct—I had changed the settings on the machine.

But he repeated Aaron's answers word-for-word.

I left the brothers in the examining room and invited their mother into my office.

"Mrs. Lester, how are the boys doing in school?"

"Aaron isn't much of a student, but he's very good at athletics."

"And Brad?"

"He seems to be doing okay."

"Does he read at home?"

"He likes comic books."

Okay, I do, too. Never could afford them as a kid, so I did some catching up in my early professional years.

"Mrs. Lester, I think Brad has a problem. Let's see if I'm right."

We re-entered the examining room just in time to stop Aaron from snapping off Brad's neck.

"Come here, Brad. Your mom says you like comic books. Would you read this for me?"

I handed him a hardbound copy of a Batman story. He turned to the first page and stared at it silently.

"Uh … Aaron's older. Can he read it first?"

I shook my head, and his expression moved to the verge of tears.

"Mrs. Lester, Brad can't read, and I think he's color blind."

Her mouth dropped.

"My father was color blind! But I don't understand. The teachers have never said anything, and he's in the fifth grade. He does so well with math, too."

Once more I played a hunch.

"Brad, let's see how well you know your numbers. If I say zero, one,

one, two, three, five, eight, what do you think the next number is?"

"Thirteen."

"And the next?"

"Twenty-one."

Without hesitation the kid had just figured out a Fibonacci sequence, adding the previous two numbers together to get the next one. Brad was an illiterate polymath, someone whose brain circuits seemed intuitively to understand numbers. He had made it to fifth grade by listening to the other children reading in class and immediately memorizing what they said.

It took a year. His mother and I drilled him in phonetics. Hesitant at first, he began to read—really read—for the first time in his life. In that one year the boy jumped from total illiteracy to high-school-level comprehension.

The ugly duckling blossomed in school, and his newly acquired confidence made him insufferable to his older brother. Happily, puberty diverted Aaron's aggressive energies elsewhere.

"Doc, do you have a computer?"

I had had some experience at university using an IBM Mark IV analog computer, which was nearly the size of a house. Now it was the dawn of the PC age, and Brad, having just turned fifteen, itched to learn how to use the devil's tool.

"We've got a surprise for you."

His mother had brought him in for a sports physical. He was into track as well as numbers.

What he didn't expect was something Mrs. Lester and I had chipped in to get for him.

"Oh, geez!"

By the time Brad graduated from high school, he had become an expert at the various arcane computer languages and had even built his own demonic device.

College brought new challenges. Brad was not an extrovert like his brother, but he had girlfriends and chugged down his share of the brew at college parties.

And, as usual, I would get the middle-of-the-night phone calls:

"Doc ... uh ... this girl ... uh ... what do I...?"

"Doc, my head is killing me. How do I stop the pounding?"

But his life revolved around math, computers—and running.

I understood his routine. My own involved 4 a.m. walks. After completing his assignments, he would change into jogging clothes and run a predetermined course around his neighborhood at night. Then, like all young adults, he would work into the early morning hours with his computers.

"Brad, I'm going to put a computer system in my office. Any suggestions?"

I had finally succumbed. Bookkeeping with a quill pen and inkwell had become a bit cumbersome, particularly because the insurance companies demanded more and more patient data.

"C'mon, Doc, we'll go visit the computer center. I'll put a system together for you."

With Brad Lester's guidance, I had joined the Information Age.

"Doc, what are you doing to that poor machine?"

"Brad, you've heard of people with green thumbs? When it comes to computers, my fingers are all thumbs."

Being a semi-moron with machinery, a modern Robert Benchley, I often called him at all hours, when the damned thing did a kluge. Somehow, magically, Brad could talk me through the labyrinth of system commands and get the Blue Screen of Death to disappear from my monitor.

That late-July evening was no different. It took almost two hours and multiple offers by Brad to come over personally, which I rejected, much to my later regret. I wanted to be able to fix the damned machine myself, albeit with his help over the phone.

We started at 9 p.m. It was 11 when my computer screen no longer spat out gibberish.

"Doc, it's time for my run. I'll call you back in an hour."

I hung up and happily typed away on the keyboard.

The phone rang a half-hour later. It was Brad's mother.

"Dr. Galen, they've arrested Brad. The police are here, and they want to search the house."

"I'll be right over."

I pulled up in front of the townhouse community where the Lesters lived. Three police cars, lights flashing blue, red, and white, sat in the parking lot. The front door of the residence was open.

An officer stopped me.

"What's your business here?"

"I'm Dr. Galen. Don't you recognize me, Bill?"

I had worked as the physician for the county jail a while back.

More on that later.

"Uh ... sorry, Doc. You related to these folks?"

"No. They're patients of mine."

He waved me in.

Brad sat on the living room couch, hands cuffed behind his back. His mother was nearly hysterical.

"There's some mistake, there's some mistake!" she kept repeating.

I approached the sergeant and showed him my ID.

"What happened?"

"We got us a Peeping Tom, Doc."

"I was just out jogging, dammit!" Brad growled.

"Tell me about it, Sergeant."

"A call came in from one of the neighborhood folks at twenty-two thirty (10:30 p.m.). Woman said there was someone looking in her front window. We got the dogs out and scoured the neighborhood. Found this guy running from us."

"Sergeant, are you sure about the time of the call?"

"Yep."

"Then you've got the wrong man. I was on the phone with Mr. Lester from twenty-one hundred to twenty-three hundred (9 to 11 p.m.)."

"Yeah, maybe so, but he was running."

"He goes jogging every night."

"The dogs went after him," the police dog-handler interjected.

"Doc, I was running and suddenly this pack of dogs came after me. What was I supposed to do?"

"We flashed our red lights at him."

"He's color blind, sergeant."

The police officer remained adamant. I could see that he wanted to close the case.

"Isn't it more likely that Mr. Lester continued to run because he was afraid of the dogs? Did any witness identify him?"

No answer. The officer tried to stare me down.

"Officer, do you have a warrant to be in Mrs. Lester's house?"

"She let us in."

I turned toward Sheila Lester.

"Did you voluntarily let the police in?"

"They said I had to let them in, Dr. Galen."

I turned back to the arresting officer. He stood his ground.

"Sorry, Doc, I still gotta take him in."

That was when Brad's true hell began. Still in handcuffs, the officers took him to the county jail and held him until bail could be posted. The judge set a trial date, when Brad refused to confess to a crime he did not commit.

I did not sleep well for days. If only I had told Brad to come over, if only...

When I finally did, it wasn't restful.

Mrs. Lester hired an attorney, and I volunteered to testify on Brad's behalf.

My secretary gave me a questioning look, when I told her not to book patients for an entire day.

"Are you sure you want to do this?"

"I have to, Virginia. The kid's innocent."

The bailiff told me to wait outside the courtroom until I was called. I didn't hear the legal foreplay, the pro forma legalese that means little but is meant to impress.

"Dr. Galen, please come in," the bailiff finally said from the open door.

I walked up to the witness stand next to the judicial throne.

Yes, I solemnly swore. I also mentally swore. The whole trial was a farce.

The defense attorney had me state my credentials and then asked the key question:

"What is your interest in this case, Doctor?"

"The officer told me that the complaint was phoned in at 10:30 p.m. At that time I was in the middle of a lengthy telephone call with Mr. Lester. It began at 9 p.m. and lasted until 11."

Like twins, the county prosecutor and the judge interjected. The judge gave way to the prosecutor.

"Dr. Galen, how can you be so sure of the time?"

"I was sitting at my desk in front of my computer screen. A two-foot diameter wall clock was directly opposite me. Besides, you can check my phone records."

"Doctor," the judge interrupted "I must warn you of the serious consequences of perjury."

Why the hell was the judge trying to intimidate me?

"I understand, Your Honor, which is why I'm telling you what I saw and heard, and when I heard it."

He told me to step down. I took a seat in the back of the courtroom.

At the end, the judge spoke those fatal words: "I find the defendant guilty."

I give the defense attorney credit for one maneuver. He asked the court to appoint a therapist to evaluate Brad, because the charge of Peeping Tom, or voyeurism, implied a mental problem. The judge agreed. It gave him a way out of a bad decision.

I approached the bench after the trial. Now I could speak.

"Your Honor," I said quietly, "this young man is innocent. Why are you doing this?"

"Dr. Galen, you're no stranger to the law. I have to work with these guys."

He gestured with his head toward the group of officers.

"Yes, Your Honor, I understand. But an innocent man has just been ruined by a sexual-deviance charge."

"Go home, Doctor."

He got up, tried to scratch his hemorrhoids without being obvious, and then left the courtroom.

He was right about one thing: I wasn't a virgin when it came to the law. One of the Three, the old doctors who had welcomed me to the area, had cured me of that.

"Dr. Bolganich is on the phone, Dr. Galen."

"Galen, my wife and I are finally taking that world cruise I promised her when we got married. Can you cover for me?"

"Sure, Nelson. Any special problems I should know about?"

"Nope, the usual stuff. Uh … oh, there's the jail, too."

As well as maintaining a private practice, Nelson was also the county-jail physician.

"Bob, I gotta warn you. It ain't like the hospital or your office."

Nelson was right.

At that time, health-care conditions at the jail facility were third-world at best. The inmate population had problems that civilians only imagined in their nightmares.

Try evaluating a female prisoner for PID (pelvic inflammatory disease), a condition that can cause permanent sterility.

The guards placed the prisoner in a cage in the middle of a floor surrounded by other cells. The guards wouldn't allow draping or covering of the open-barred walls for privacy. The only concession was that I was allowed to place a sheet over her, as I attempted a pelvic examination, while the other inmates jeered, and the guards cracked lewd jokes.

But that paled in comparison with the legal Kabuki dance of serving on medical-malpractice committees.

As Nelson handed me the keys to his office, he gave me a guilty look.

"Uh ... Bob, I've got a panel I need you to cover for me."

The state, in an attempt to decrease the time and expense of medical-malpractice trials, had set up a legal process, in which a panel of three doctors, three lawyers, and a judge would pre-screen complaints of medical misconduct. If the panel decided that the doctor was guilty, then they offered both plaintiff and defendant the choice of an out-of-court settlement or the prospect of a trial. If they deemed the doctor innocent, the hoped-for outcome was the dropping of the case against him, or her.

What actually took place was a mini-trial.

The plaintiff's attorneys used it as practice to test their strategies. The panel decision made no difference.

Yes, indeed, I was no legal virgin. But for some strange, foolish altruism, I still believed justice would be served.

Three months after Brad Lester's trial, he reappeared before the judge who had convicted him. He had faithfully attended the weekly sessions at the therapist's office. The court-appointed psychologist presented his report in the open courtroom.

"I find no evidence for a diagnosis of sexual deviance. This man is innocent."

The judge stared at him, then at Brad Lester, and then shook his head.

"Thank you, Dr. Siemens, but my decision stands. I will, however, suspend jail time, provided that Mr. Lester continues to attend therapy sessions for one year."

"But, your honor, that would be a waste of time," Siemens interjected.

"Mr. Lester has a choice. He can attend sessions at your office or go to jail for one year."

Then the latter-day Pontius Pilate rose from the bench and left the courtroom.

On one level I understood the judge's hard line. At the time this legal travesty occurred, other, more serious and devastating witch trials were taking place across the country.

Charges of sexual perversion in schools and daycare centers, led by therapists needing an outlet for their own neuroses, had resulted in people being charged with extreme perversions: demon worship, naked cabals with infants, and more.

Reacting to the outrage, judges and prosecutors abandoned reason in the name of expediency … and votes.

Sorry to say, I had experienced something similar during my own boyhood.

"Pepe, don't do it!"

"Padre Luis said it was God's will, Berto."

My friend Sal and I were standing on the bridge overpass, the same one where the dead lady had met me seven years before, caught underneath on one of its pylons. We were both fifteen years old at the time, and boys through and through. Pepe sometimes hung out with us, when his other friends were away.

"Pepe, get down from there. Are you *loco*?"

Sal and I stared, wide-eyed, as the boy climbed up on the bridge wall and paced back and forth before stopping and staring down at the river.

We thought it was a joke. Then I saw the tears in his eyes. He was going to jump.

I motioned with a hand behind my back. I would try to distract him. Sal would grab him and pull him down.

I leaned against the concrete and looked up at the young Chicano.

"What happened, Pepe? Is your baby sister driving you nuts?"

I had helped Dr. Agnelli deliver his little sister a month before.

"Padre Luis, he said it was all right."

He bowed his head and closed his eyes.

"Now, Sal!"

The strongest kid in the neighborhood grabbed Pepe's legs and pulled. Both fell backwards onto the sidewalk, with Pepe landing on top. Sal jumped up, and the boy lay spread-eagle on the ground, an olive-skinned angel crying uncontrollably.

"Why, Pepe?"

We sat down next to him, and a torrent of horror flowed from his lips.

He had been sexually molested by a local pastor who had called the act "God's will."

Sal and I had attended the parochial grammar school, so our knuckles had felt the wrath of numerous nuns and their rulers in our earlier years. But we had never experienced anything untoward. And, like Pepe, we had been taught to respect the representatives of God on Earth.

They were crusty old men who brooked no nonsense.

That didn't stop Papa, also crusty, from passing on to me one of his pearls of wisdom: Never take marital advice from a man wearing skirts. It took me a while to understand what he meant.

Then a new pastor arrived at the parish, after the older priest had passed away. By then Sal and I had moved on to high school. Sal, never one for religion, had long since given up on churchgoing. I was now involved with Concepción High School and its own parish. Neither of us had any contact with or knowledge of the new priest.

"Come on, Pepe, I'm taking you home."

Sal pulled the boy to his feet. He looked at me, and I understood.

It was late afternoon, when I walked up the steps of the church, where I had gotten so many calluses from kneeling. I entered the vestibule and opened the door leading to the church proper. There was an unfamiliar priest rearranging the votive candles in the racks near the altar railing.

I moved slowly up the side aisle.

"Are you Father Luis?"

"Yes. I don't recognize you, my son. Are you new here?"

"I'm Berto. Do you know Pepe Rodriguez?"

His face started to twitch.

"Father Luis, Pepe just tried to kill himself. Do you want to know why?"

He turned from me, but I grabbed his left shoulder and turned him back around.

I wasn't as strong as Sal, but I was angry—angrier than I had ever been before.

"Why, Father?"

He extended his right hand and patted me on the cheek.

I hauled off and cold-cocked him.

"You're going to Hell for striking a man of God!"

"Padre, if I do, you'll be waiting for me at the gates."

I turned and walked out.

Pepe killed himself a week later. Oh, they said it was gang-related, but Pepe had never belonged to any of the gangs and, like Sal and me, he avoided the altercations on Hamilton Street.

Sal and I knew it was suicide by gang fight.

Brad Lester?

He was never the same. Even as he attended the weekly and unnecessary psych sessions, he withdrew into a paranoid state. He became a top-notch computer expert, but his personal life was shot.

The judge?

He was murdered by his own, drug-addicted son. The young man dissected him with a ceremonial sword, because his father had stopped supporting his habit.

Justice?

Maybe my Catechism was right: It's reserved for the Lord.

In this life it seems a rare commodity, indeed.

Consequences

"Dr. Galen, Dr. Maitland is on line one."

"Hey, George, what's up?"

He was the only one left.

The big, ex-Army Air Corps pilot and physician had turned seventy-nine a week earlier. He had been retired from office practice for ten years, when Joe Grasso, the eldest member of the Three, had suffered a series of small strokes that ended his physical and mental ability to practice medicine.

It was one of the most difficult duties that George Maitland and Nelson Bolganich—and I, for that matter—had to undertake: telling a colleague and close friend to hang it up, to stop being a doctor.

I remember the look in Joe's eyes, conveying a deep sense of loss and betrayal. His remaining mental faculties could barely contain the reality of the situation. Then, a short time later, a bigger stroke took him, and he was gone.

It had hit Nelson the hardest. He broke into tears after Joe's funeral, repeating over and over that he wanted to die with his boots on, not in little pieces like Joe's mind.

He got his wish—a massive heart attack hit him at breakfast three years later.

At the time, he could only wear one boot. The other leg had been amputated because of unstoppable diabetic changes in his circulation.

Now it was just George Maitland—and me.

"Bob, I've put your name in to replace me on the advisory staff. I'm getting a bit long in the tooth."

"You sure about this, George?"

He had achieved great success after taking over Joe Grasso's position. The hospital's mentoring program for internists was one of the best in the country.

I could hear the hesitation in his voice.

"Bob, it's not been the same since my Marla..."

His wife of fifty two-years had passed away recently.

I knew how he felt.

"Tell you what, George. I'll stop by your office about six tonight. How about we discuss it then?"

"Sure. Uh ... can I ask one favor?"

"Shoot."

"We've got a sticky situation. I'm supposed to chair a meeting this afternoon. It's about Crescenzi and Galkis. That damned luddite McKaylic wants them out of the program."

"What's his beef with them? You said they were two of the best students you ever had. No one's complained about them, and the nursing staff can't stop gushing over their work."

I knew George too well not to pick up on his reluctance.

"Bob, they're ... uh ... lovers. McKaylic claims that falls under the moral-turpitude clause."

"I never saw any objectionable behavior in the hospital."

"Neither have I. Most of the problems I've dealt with involve male students and female nurses or female students and male attendings."

"So where's McKaylic coming from?"

"Apparently these two guys share an apartment near his house. He claims he saw them kissing and holding hands early last Sunday on his way to church."

Liam McKaylic was one of those fussy people whose sole mission in life was to make other people as miserable as he was. If they'd ever remade the movie *People Will Talk* he'd have been a perfect Professor Elwell—no acting required.

"Were they out in public?"

"Here's the funny part. McKaylic says he was watching them from his bedroom window. The two guys have one of those apartments with a sliding-glass back door, and their yard faces his backyard. Wouldn't surprise me if he was using binoculars."

"George, it's none of his damned business what the kids do outside the hospital, as long as it's not against the law."

"Bob, I'm in full agreement. That's why I want you to chair the meeting. It'll be you, McKaylic, and I've asked Ben Jacoby to be the third on the committee. I know he thinks McKaylic's a pompous, self-righteous ass. For one thing, McKaylic actually tried to put the make on Jacoby's wife a while back."

"Okay, I'll do it. When's the meeting?"

"It's at 4 o'clock."

"Hold on a sec."

I yelled out to Barbara. She told me from 3:30 on was clear.

"It's a go, George. I'll stop by your office after we're done."

He thanked me and hung up.

I stared at the wall.

I won't let it happen again.

I closed my eyes.

"Berto, Berto, wait up!"

"Whaddya want, Nicky? I gotta make my rounds?"

The boy was shy. Medium height and pencil-thin, his long eyelashes highlighted dark-brown eyes and glistening black hair. He flashed pearly white teeth in a smile, as he caught up with me and patted me on the shoulder.

"*Si, Dottore* Berto, I know, I know."

"Well...?"

"Can I go with you?"

The New Jersey tenement where I grew up sat in the middle of an ethnic and religious stewpot of nation-neighborhoods. Like today's world, each of them established inviolate territorial lines. If you belonged to one group, you didn't cross over into the neighborhood of another's, unless you were foolhardy or stupid—or me.

I can still see Nicky's face, hesitant yet hopeful.

"Okay, but keep your mouth shut and stay next to me. Don't go wandering off."

"Mum's the word, *Dottore*. I'm here to learn."

We walked to the east end of our world and crossed an invisible boundary into another, one inhabited by strangers who spoke in heavy, harsh consonants and languages predating the birth of Jesus. As in any war zone, sentries watched the border.

But I was different—they didn't stop me.

No, it wasn't because I was the meanest son-of-a-bitch on the block. Other pretenders to that throne had been laid to rest in the town's cemetery.

Through good fortune and early flashes of wisdom, I chose to be useful to all sides.

I can still see the blood pouring from the groin of the young man lying on Hamilton Street. I was ten and proudly wore the brass belt-buckle proclaiming my name, BERTO. I can still hear myself calling out to my friends.

"Tomas, go get a bottle of your papa's *vino*. Angelo, get a needle from your mama's sewing kit—quick!"

My first patient was a gang member who had suffered a femoral artery puncture from a switchblade. I pressed on that artery then stitched it back together using needle and thread from Angelo's mom, while he took over the pressure.

It worked.

After that, I attended the war casualties for the five neighborhoods. Whenever a young tough got knifed or zip-gunned, they called me. Nobody stopped me, and no one tried to rough me up. I was protected. I was *Dottore* Berto.

After George's call, I couldn't shake off the flood of memories.

"Hey, Berto, you hangin' 'roun with fags now?"

"Goddam queer!"

"Get the hell outta here, D'Angelo!"

"Lousy *feygelah* bastard!"

The insults and epithets continued, but we kept walking, unmolested.

"Nicky, what the hell did you do to these guys?"

"I offend them by being alive, Berto."

I watched, as Nicky D'Angelo's delicate face flushed. Nicky D. wasn't telling me the whole truth, but I let it drop. I had work to do.

We arrived at the stoop of one of the countless, drab, aging buildings in that part of Newark, and I found my patient lying on the steps.

"Berto, that's Mutanov!"

Nicky tried to back away, but I grabbed his arm and whispered, "You've gotta help me. You run now, you know what'll happen."

A crowd of the injured guy's friends had formed a semicircle around us. I examined the twenty-something gang leader. Someone had slashed his forearm open. I could deal with it, because I had spent a great deal of time at the neighborhood free clinic run by my mentor, Dr. Agnelli. Images of his skilled hands treating patients with similar injuries flashed through my head and guided me, as I tested the nerve and muscle function in the injured tough's limb.

"Mika, I can clean this and close it, but you'll need to stop by Agnelli's place for a tetanus shot. Understand? Don't worry about the cops. He doesn't have to report tetanus shots."

Pitch-black eyes stared up at me, and he mumbled a "ya," accompanied by a nod.

"Nicky, hand me that little bottle with the needle in it then pour some *vino* over the wound.

"Mika, this is gonna sting."

D'Angelo followed my directions well, and the repair job went smoothly.

"Don't forget, Mika, go to Agnelli's tomorrow and get that shot."

My errand of mercy completed, we walked away from the crowd of toughs. After a block or so, Nicky patted me on the shoulder. Hesitantly, he blurted out, "Can we stop by . . .?"

He mentioned a building in the direction we were headed. I didn't think anything of it, so I agreed.

Different block, same building style: dirty, ugly tenement.

"Wait here, Berto."

Nicky entered the building, and I cooled my heels for what seemed like forever.

When he walked back out, another boy, also about sixteen, accompanied him.

"Berto, this is my friend, Constantin Bierkov."

The other boy held out his hand, and I shook it.

"Call me Stan," he said.

"Nicky, we need to get moving. Nice meeting you, Stan."

I was fourteen then, two years younger than Nicky. The other kids his age didn't hang out with him. Instead, he often tagged along with me and, somehow, we always finished our rounds at Stan's place.

What happened next I will carry to my dying day.

"Hey, Berto. Why you let that creep Nicky D. hang around with you?"

I was walking with the emissary from another territory, who had summoned me for help with one of his gang.

"What's wrong with him, Tiny?"

Tiny stood over six feet tall and weighed close to three-hundred pounds.

"Don't tell me you don't know."

"Know what?"

"He's an effin' queer."

"Huh?"

"Yeah, he's usin' you to see his sweetheart—that kid Stan."

I turned red and, holding my breath, started to tremble. I felt betrayed. I had actually thought Nicky D. wanted to learn to help people. He seemed to pick up on things quickly, and he was a good assistant, but Tiny was right—Nicky had been using me.

I didn't know how to handle this.

The next time I saw Nicky, I told him he couldn't accompany me anymore on my rounds.

"Stay away from me, Nicky. Just stay away from me."

"Please, Berto. Don't do this to me. Please!"

I watched him burst into tears—and I walked away.

I was too young to understand. Back then everything was black or white. There were no shades of gray. I couldn't have fathomed how overwhelming love could be.

Yet, I felt the need to seek counsel; to understand my own decision.

I had to tell someone, and it couldn't be one of my friends. I walked past the little shop run by Thomas the Barber. It was closed. I found him a few doors down in Mr. Ruddy's shoe shop. Two of the three Old Guys were there as well.

"Come on in, kid," Mr. Ruddy said.

"Ya, you come in, Berto," Thomas added.

Harold Ruddy, the half-bodied Yoda, studied me. Those piercing, blue eyes were never wrong.

"What's eating you, Berto?"

I hoisted myself up on the counter and shrugged my shoulders.

"Hey, kid," said Mr. Huff. "You got a monkey on your back as big and ugly as old Thomas here."

George Huff, still haunted by the ghosts of World War I shellshock, could surprise me with spontaneous humor.

I told them what had happened.

Mr. Ruddy sucked in his breath, and even Thomas muttered a "merde."

"Berto, don't do this to Nicky," Mr. Huff exclaimed.

"But . . . but . . . why not?" I stammered. "He was using me. And he's a . . ."

Thomas's massive arms grabbed me and shook me. He had never before spoken an angry word to me.

"You have signed Nicky's death warrant."

"Berto, you know better. Think, boy!"

Mr. Ruddy stared at me. They all did.

Oh, God!

A multitude of feelings assaulted me, right on the coattails of a forcefully suppressed memory. I remembered how I had felt, when my girlfriend Bernice was transferred to another school, because a damned nun hated blacks. That episode has haunted me for decades as well.

The Old Guys saw the realization in my face, when they confronted me with the meaning of my action towards Nicky.

"Good, you see now, don't you, boy?" Mr. Ruddy asked. "Some things should never be forgotten."

That was my cue. I ran out of the shop. I had to find Nicky.

What I had forgotten was the jungle grapevine, which, like me, respected no boundaries. The neighborhood toughs soon learned that Nicky D'Angelo was no longer under my protection.

"Hey, Nicky, Stan's hurt. Berto's with him, but he's callin' for ya."

"Take me to him, Tiny . . . please!"

The big guy laughed and patted Nicky's head.

"Sure, sure, kid. I'll take you."

They had lured Nicky and Stan to an out-of-the-way alley.

My friend Sal had found me before I could find Nicky.

"Berto, somethin's goin' down with Nicky D. and Stan. Tiny's been going around saying he's gonna fix things up, and I saw him off territory near Nicky's street. You better get over there and talk to that big palooka."

We ran. Sal, as big and strong as he was, would not have ventured into that other world without me.

"Oh, jeez, Berto!"

Sal reached the end of the alley first. He retched at what he saw, and he tried to stop me from going farther.

But I saw them lying there. We had chosen the alley as a shortcut and by sheer chance found Tiny's handiwork. Nicky and Stan had been stripped and sexually mutilated with knives. They were still alive.

A merciful God would have taken them.

A short time later the ambulance took them away.

A few days afterward, I was hanging out at Dr. Agnelli's clinic—the only place where I could find solace. Corrado shook his head, when I told him what had happened. His dark eyes couldn't look at me, and he didn't say anything.

Then one of his nurses stuck her head through the open door.

"Dr. Agnelli..."

She noticed me.

"You'd better take this call."

He picked up the old, heavy, black, Bakelite phone, and his eyebrows rose then creased in an inverted V. He hung up without saying a word and turned to me.

"Berto … Nicky and Stan … I'm sorry."

They had held hands and jumped off the roof of the hospital just before being sent home.

Not all Romeos and Juliets are boys and girls.

The mood of that tortuous reverie haunted me, as I walked into the hospital meeting room. The two medical students—Crescenzi and Galkis—sat outside in the hallway.

They watched me go past silently. I guess the look on my face scared them. Crescenzi reached over and held the other young man's hand.

Jacoby and McKaylic were sitting at the table, waiting.

"Galen, I didn't know bears worked in hospitals."

Jacoby was trying to defuse a bad situation. He had been alone for some time with McKaylic. Neither man liked the other.

I sat down. McKaylic was scowling.

"Hello, Liam, Ben."

Both men nodded.

"Liam, I didn't know you liked Indian food," I said.

Ben's eyebrows rose. McKaylic didn't reply.

"Yeah, next time you and … your … uh … wife … stop by Soufi Delight, try the mooli bread. I can't get enough of it."

Ben allowed himself a slight smile.

"Yeah, Galen, it shows," he said, dryly.

McKaylic was turning beet red.

I cleared my throat.

"Let's get down to business. What's the story?"

"Those two should be dismissed from the program."

"What two, Liam?"

"Crescenzi and Galkis. They're a disgrace to the hospital. They're..."

"What seems to be the problem?" Ben interjected.

"You know damned well what."

I stared at the bald-headed, little man.

"No, tell us, Liam."

"They were ... uh ... you know."

"No, I don't. And if my memory serves me, that wasn't your wife having dinner with you the other night. Does the missus know about your office nurse?"

Ben couldn't control himself. He turned to McKaylic.

"So, you've been naughty again, Liam? Does Della know?"

McKaylic's expression darkened. His voice slipped into an accented patois.

"You bloody bastards, who are you to criticize me!"

"I'm glad you asked, Liam," Ben drawled. "I think you're a lowdown son-of-a-bitch for sniffing around my wife like some dog in heat."

I started piling on.

"And what about you and that medical student ... what was her name ... Angela? As I recall she filed a complaint against you for sexual harassment, and you went out of your way to libel her. Didn't you even write to her school dean without the permission of this hospital?"

"She was a damned whore! The little bitch! She came on to me."

"That's not the way the nurses and house staff saw it. Besides, you don't have the looks for anyone who isn't blind to come on to you."

McKaylic kicked his chair backward and lunged at me.

That was, shall we say, a major tactical mistake.

Suddenly I was reliving my college days. My right hand shot out and grabbed his scrawny neck. Only Ben's shout stopped me from clamping down on his windpipe.

"Bob, no! He's not worth it!"

I released my grip. McKaylic fell back into his chair, holding his throat and gasping. He tried to speak, but his hoarse voice was barely audible.

"I'll sue you for this, you fat bastard! I'll sue you both!"

"You were the one who went for Galen," Ben countered. "Besides, I don't think your wife and patients would like to see the parade of female students and nurses who would be more than happy to testify against you. Imagine everyone finding out that the student you harassed tried to kill herself, because you maligned her. Damned good thing her resident got to her in time. Lucky for you we convinced her dean there was no substance to your allegations, just like there's no cause for action against those two kids out in the hallway."

I had calmed down some. I stared at McKaylic, laser-like.

"Look, Liam, here's the bottom line: We're not going to let you slander those two talented young men because of your neuroses. You got that?"

By the time McKaylic had sputtered a few unintelligibles and gotten himself up and out of the room, Ben was shooting me a mile-wide grin.

"You got a way with words, Galen."

"Yup, sometimes. So, you think we got enough on that bastard to get him kicked off the staff?"

"I'll see what the executive committee and the legal counsel have to say."

"Meeting adjourned?"

He just smiled again.

When I walked out of the room, Crescenzi and Galkis stood up apprehensively.

"Why the hell are you two still here?" I growled. "Don't you have patients to take care of?"

Crescenzi understood immediately.

"Dr. Galen ... uh ... I ... we..."

As Ben joined us, Galkis held out his hand.

"Thanks, Dr. Galen, Dr. Jacoby."

They turned and practically ran down the hall to their ward duties.

"Galen, you heard what drove me in there, but what's your demon?"

"It's a long story. For now, let's just say this was my attempt to atone for an old but grave mistake."

He nodded and left for another committee meeting.

I headed to the stairwell entrance and climbed up one flight. George Maitland's office was halfway down the corridor.

The door was ajar, and only a small desk lamp lit the room.

I stuck my head in and called, "Hey, George, problem solved!"

No response.

Then I saw my friend. He slumped in his chair, motionless, his late wife's picture lying across his chest. His eyes were half-open, and a smile graced his lifeless face.

I already knew, but I had to go through the motions.

I felt his cold skin and detected no pulse in his neck.

I opened my bag and took out my stethoscope. I listened to his chest.

Again, nothing.

I closed his eyes.

I sat down in a side chair, my eyes clouded with tears.

The old Army Air Corps pilot had fought his last dogfight.

But the Dark Angel had won.

Circles

The mind is like a parachute. It works best when open.

—author unknown

"Doc, I leave for school tomorrow."

We sat in my back yard. The contrast wasn't hard to see.

I was getting older, maybe a little more cynical than necessary.

The young man sitting across from me pretended worldliness, but his body language conveyed palpable fear and uncertainty. Yet there was an eagerness about him that made me . . . envious?

When had I lost that spark?

I had seen it in my colleagues. We call it physician burnout. The rising demands of outside parties and influences—government agencies, insurance companies, and popular misconceptions about what doctors could do—sooner or later take their toll.

Loss of autonomy is hell for someone who has had to make independent decisions his or her entire life.

I stood up and stretched.

"Come on, Rick. We can talk while we walk, okay?"

Richard Shepland III nodded and rose.

"Doc, I gotta admit, it scares me. I've busted my rump just to get to this moment, and now I'm scared."

"You remember how you felt when you got married?"

"Yeah."

"Was it worth it?"

He grinned.

"Best damned thing I ever did. Patty's kept me focused. She shares my dream. God, I'm lucky!"

I stared out at my garden. The small memorial plots I had planted years ago in memory of my Leni and Cathy were in full bloom. The daylilies and Hibiscus cast their whites, reds, chocolates, and yellows against a teal-blue sky.

Oh, how I miss you both.

"Did you say something, Doc?"

"Uh ... no, Rick, just clearing my throat ... ahem. So, your tuition is covered, and you have enough money to survive while Patty settles into her new job in Richmond, yes?"

"Yeah, thanks, Doc."

"Good. What about your apartment?"

"It's walking distance from school. You gonna come visit?"

"I might. You guys have a spare room?"

"Yeah, but..."

Thought so.

"Uh ... Doc, can I tell you something personal?"

"You're not pregnant, are you Rick?"

He flashed a smile.

"No, but Patty is."

You sure have taken on a helluva load, haven't you, boy?

"Congratulations! Now, how did that happen? I thought we had the birds-and-bees talk when you were fourteen."

He blushed.

"Remember how you keep telling me that ... uh ... stuff happens?"

Not quite the word I would use, but his version was cleaner.

"I see your point. Is that what you wanted to tell me?"

"Part of it."

He paused.

"Doc, would you think less of me if I told you I was scared shitless?"

Once again, that mantle of fear arose.

"About becoming a father?"

"All of it. I just kinda feel trapped … you know … marriage, school, baby on the way. How'm I gonna do it?"

"I don't know, Rick, you just do."

He looked at me quizzically.

"I used to ask myself the same questions. Then I visited my mentor, Dr. Agnelli, and asked how he did it. Know what he told me?"

Rick shook his head.

"He looked me right in the eye and said, 'If this life is for you, you just do it, and don't ever look back.'"

"Why not?"

"Because, your personal demons might just catch you. Besides, you'll be so busy, you won't have time to worry."

He smiled.

"One more question, Doc."

"Shoot."

"You ever make any mistakes … I mean, big ones?"

Mistakes!

I stared at the backs of my hands, now beginning to mottle and thin, a parchment testimony of time's passage. Were these really the hands that had caressed and loved? Were they the same hands that had moved over countless, fearful bodies, feeling the river of life flow strongly in some and at ebb tide in others? Hands and fingers, seeking, searching out what should be and what should not, guiding my eyes, ears, and mind toward a decision—a conclusion.

Sometimes those hands were wrong.

I motioned Rick over to the twin benches on the lawn, and we sat down. Light breezes rippled the air, and several geese and ducks idled in flight along the edge of the sky, eyes closed in the midday warmth.

I rubbed my knees.

"If you didn't already have wavy hair, I could tell you stories that would curl every last one on your head. Now, listen up, boy. If I can impart only one bit of wisdom to you, it's this: Your patients will tell you their diagnosis."

I noticed the tension leaving the young man's shoulders. The crease of a smile replaced the clenched jaw of anxiety. Good! That was what I had hoped to accomplish.

At least I hadn't lost my way with words.

So the boy/man sat, cross-legged, on the bench across from me, looking like an expectant puppy.

All right, Grasshopper, let Master Po tell you how much of a screw-up he once was…

It was one of those days that started out normally—though I received the first phone call at 5 a.m., after my usual, early morning walk.

"Dr. Galen?"

"Yes, Mrs. Meland."

"It's Seth, he's still crying."

It was unusual for Sylvia Meland not to call.

Seth was her first child. He was only two months old, but he had been miserable since day one: eczema, reflux, digestive problems, and colic. The multiple lab studies I had ordered all came back normal, and the pediatricians I had consulted said it probably was the luck of the draw: Seth was just a colicky baby.

Nevertheless, at least once a week, Sylvia would bring Seth in and show me diapers filled with the normal, pasty-yellow movements of a breastfed baby.

"Is this really normal?"

I tried to be supportive. I understood that first babies were a new mother's most trying experience. So each visit I would look Seth over, weigh him, and run my hands over his head, neck, and abdomen. And every visit I would see and find nothing out of the ordinary.

But that particular morning, Sylvia Meland arrived at my door at 6:30. She was in tears, holding the screaming infant in her outstretched hands.

"I can't take it any longer!"

The same words crossed my own mind.

"Mrs. Meland, I still can't find anything."

"Please, Dr. Galen, please put him in the hospital!"

I didn't want to do it. Call it ego, call it dread of unnecessary hospital admissions and looking bad in front of my peers. But the way things were going, if Seth weren't hospitalized for evaluation, his mother soon would be. She had drawn very close to a nervous breakdown.

I called the admitting desk and made the arrangements; then I called a colleague, a top-of-the-line pediatrician.

"Don't you ever sleep, Bob?"

"Only the good sleep, Tom. You know that."

"Yeah, that's why you woke me up. Whatcha got?"

I ran through Seth's story, and Tom Paulson interrupted me several times with an, "Are you sure it isn't just really bad colic?"

Finally he agreed to examine the baby.

So Sylvia took Seth out to the car and drove to the hospital. She seemed relieved. If nothing else her baby would be taken off her hands for a while.

Then the guilt hit me. I realized that I simply had grown tired of hearing her cry wolf day after day. And I understood that I now felt the same way about her as she did about Seth.

The day progressed as I expected. There were the usual back pains, headaches, and runny noses. Then I met Alex.

"Wanna see someone on your lunch hour?" Barbara called back from the reception desk.

"Why?"

"Parents say their kid's arms and legs don't work right."

The Daumiers were what you might call citizens of the world. Representing our government in numerous countries over the years, they had just returned from Europe and were still setting up house nearby.

Their Alex was fourteen and all boy. But when they brought him in, he stumbled down the hall, even though they were supporting both his arms.

"What happened, Alex?"

"I fell."

"And..."

"He was practicing for a merit badge for his boy scout troop. He had to climb a tree to demonstrate limb-cutting."

"I slipped."

"How far did you fall?"

"Twenty, maybe twenty-five feet."

"Mrs. Daumier, Alex needs to go immediately to the hospital."

"We just came from there. They said he only had bruises and discharged him. On the ride back, he started to complain about pain then numbness in both his arms and legs."

I grabbed a cervical (neck) brace from my closet and put it on the boy. Then I did a quick check of his reflexes and his response to different sensations on the skin of his arms and legs. Muscle-strength testing showed marked loss of his ability to flex.

Alex Daumier had suffered spinal-cord trauma. His parents were thinking he had received a minor injury. But I knew it was already a fifty-fifty chance he would become paralyzed.

I called the rescue squad and put in a call to a neurosurgeon.

"What's the story, Bob?"

We exchanged information on Alex's medical status in the typical staccato, code lingo doctors use to communicate with each other fast.

"I'll meet him in the ER. Good call, Bob."

While we waited for the ambulance, I sat down with the Daumiers.

"Sometimes this type of fall—the impact from it—causes tissue swelling around the base of the brain and spinal cord. In Alex's case, the injury is in his neck. That would explain why he has both arm and leg symptoms. The wires that give feeling and the ability to move start at the top and move downward. Put pressure at the top and you can affect any or all levels of function."

The ambulance siren echoed through the office, as I finished. The EMTs rushed in with their cart. They slipped a board under Alex and carefully positioned him on it then inserted two IVs—much to the boy's dismay.

I gave them a quick rundown, making sure they understood that the neurosurgeon was waiting at the hospital.

Two hours later I got the call.

"We got him—just in time," my colleague said. "He was starting to lose sphincter control (bladder and bowel). He's on high-dose dex (dexamethasone, a steroid used to reduce swelling quickly)."

"Many thanks, Ron. I'll be by this evening."

I looked over the appointment book on my secretary's desk. The rest of the afternoon was routine: chest pains, difficulty breathing, headaches. Then I spotted the last name scheduled: Tom Regelson.

I had treated Tom and his family—actually two families—for a number of years, and the wordplay and literary discussions I had enjoyed with him became a favorite part of my day-to-day routine.

Tom was a retired college professor, a transplanted Minnesotan, who had become a world-renowned expert in Sinology. He was expert in other Asian languages and cultures as well.

And he was a deeply religious man, heavily involved in his church activities. Retirement allowed him to delve deeper into the philosophical mysteries that drive all thoughtful people. Tom had no doubt there was an afterlife, but his keen intellect and overwhelming rationality could not refrain from seeking causality.

Good, I thought, *get through the day and see what Professor Tom will bring up next.*

Five o'clock approached. I was standing by my secretary's desk finishing some chart work, when I saw Tom's Ichabod Crane figure coming up the walk.

"Virginia, it's time to call it a day. I'll wrap up after seeing Dr. Regelson. You head on home."

She gave me "the look." She knew how much I enjoyed the verbal jousting that would soon ensue—and she knew some of it wouldn't be fit for her genteel ears.

I opened the door just as Tom reached it, and I was about to welcome him in, when he beat me to it.

"*Ni hao ma,* good doctor."

I attempted to reply, "*Hao hen,*" and he laughed at my grossly mispronounced Chinese, as he followed me into the exam room.

I performed some precursive checks and sat down. But what followed surprised the hell out of me.

"I've been thinking about you and your career," he said. "Actually we were talking about you at the club."

He mentioned the name of a very exclusive enclave in Washington for people of world accomplishment.

"Good doctor, have you ever thought of writing about your experiences in the medical profession? I know some of the stories we've talked about. You've seen aspects of people that most of us can only imagine. Have you ever considered keeping a diary?"

"Tom, I don't feel like either a Boswell or a Johnson, and I'm no Erasmus Darwin, either. What on earth would I be able to write about that would be of interest to anyone else?"

"Why not write about yourself?"

I couldn't help it; I laughed out loud. I should write about the sordid details of my stream of patients? Who would want to read about that—Jerry Springer?

"Think it over, young doctor," Tom replied. Then he launched us into a discussion of 1940s *film noir* and the literary values of Golden Age radio. An hour passed, before we decided to call it quits.

I grabbed a quick bite then headed to the hospital. The neurosurgery wing was nearest, so I stuck my head in room 503 to check on Alex.

He didn't need my attention. Half the nurses were standing around his bed, as the fourteen-year-old boy flirted like a pro.

Must have been the dexamethasone.

Right.

The infant ward was quiet. I went to the unit secretary's carrel and grabbed Seth Meland's chart.

"Bob."

"Hey, Tom."

"Uh … listen, that baby, Seth? He's got a problem."

My stomach knotted. What had I missed? I asked Paulson point blank.

"Bad?"

He nodded.

"Tom, I couldn't find anything."

"He's got leukemia."

Suddenly I had to sit down. My legs felt weak. Tom sat with me.

"But his last lab was only three weeks ago. It was normal!"

"It's bad, Bob—AML. Comes on like a tornado."

Acute myeloid leukemia. Even today, with bone-marrow transplants and other forms of chemotherapy, it remains a terrible diagnosis. And the worst prognosis is for babies under one year of age.

"Think that was making him so fussy?"

"Hard to tell. Usually doesn't present that way."

"Does his mother know?"

"Yeah."

He paused.

"Bob, I'm not sure how to put this, but she actually seems relieved."

We sat there and stared at the wall.

It was late September, following a summer when the thermometer had caused those who doubted global warming to doubt their doubts. The usual run of preschool and college physicals had ended, and kids who had reveled in classroom-free abandon now made plans to display their athletic prowess in sports tryouts. Even my Saturdays were booked up with hopeful football players and cheerleader wannabes.

Ever since Cathy had passed away, I worked the weekends alone.

The phone rang. I was pleased to hear Tom Regelson's voice.

"Do you have some free time, young doctor?"

"Of course. Come on down. Any problems?"

"Probably a minor one, but I'd like it checked out."

Waiting for Tom I signed a sports-physical form and handed it to the ninety-pound, fourteen-year-old boy who desperately wanted to be a linebacker. He strutted out of the office accompanied by two friends, trying to flex his muscles.

Several minutes later I saw Tom's classic Porsche pull into my lot. He got out and walked slowly toward my door. I noticed it immediately. The man was not the same, and he lacked his normally confident stride. The Ichabod Crane figure truly appeared haunted by the Headless Horseman.

"Come on back, Tom."

He leaned against the exam table and abruptly said, "I think I have cancer."

"What makes you think so?"

"The left side of my face feels different."

"What do you mean?"

"It feels like there's something growing in there."

"How long?"

"About two weeks."

My fingers moved, as usual, with a mind of their own—pressing, palpating, playing the keyboard of a man's life under their pads. I scanned my mental database of causalities. Was it a change in the way the nerve supplied feeling to the area? That would have been the best reason. Bell's palsy was a self-limited condition.

No, the pattern wasn't right. There was no drooping on one side of the face or eyelid. That also helped to exclude brain damage of the stroke kind.

I palpated the glands that helped produce saliva: parotid, sublingual, submaxillary. I couldn't feel any discreet enlargement. Then I put on gloves and examined the same glands from within the patient's mouth. Still nothing.

"Tom, why do you think it's cancer?"

"Remember when I had that abnormal skin spot on the left side of my face? You thought it was malignant and sent me to the dermatologist. He removed it and said it was squamous cancer."

My eyes closed involuntarily. Yes, it was possible. But this fast? Most likely it was an irritation of the big saliva gland, the parotid—yes, that would be it.

"Tom, if you go by the numbers this is a gland inflammation. Let's try a short course of medication. If there's no relief, then we'll get some imaging studies."

"I don't want to wait."

"Give it the weekend. If there's no change, we'll get an MRI on Monday."

He agreed and left.

My intuition—call it my gut—was warning me: Tom would be phoning on Monday.

And so it happened.

I arranged for an MRI, and the device spun the water molecules in Tom's body in an atomic line-dance to reveal what the old professor already knew in his heart: cancer—cancer of the parotid gland, which had spread to lymph nodes in his neck. It was rare, but Tom would probably be right about the type of cancer, too.

Now began the *danse macabre* of tissue-typing, staging, and excision. The surgeon's hands moved about the traffic circle of nerves, glands, and blood vessels compacted around the front and base of the left ear. He attempting to preserve feeling and function in Tom's face while removing the crab that wanted to take his life.

It was a tribute to the surgeon's skill—and the patient's will—that a week after major surgery, Tom Regelson was up and moving as if nothing had happened.

But he was no fool. He had done his homework and understood this was just the beginning. Now the fight to prevent or minimize spread by use of radiation therapy began. It would not be pleasant, and the side effects were potentially serious.

Tom never stopped coming by my office on the weekends to apprise me of his condition. And week by week I could see the effects of the demon monkey that rode his soul. I couldn't imagine what his powerful intellect did to him during those quiet hours, when rest was supposed to purge the body of its daily buildup of physical and psychic toxins.

"Tom, how are you holding up?"

"I've become even closer to my studies on the origins and basis of faith, young doctor, and—yes, to answer your unspoken question—at times I am afraid."

We looked at each other in silent understanding...

"Doc?"

"Oh, sorry. Rick. Guess I got lost in thought."

I stared at my surroundings. I was in my back yard, talking to the young, soon-to-be medical student.

"So, what happened to the professor and Alex and baby Seth?"

He watched me intently. I had been staring off into a distant past. I rose and walked to the edge of the yard and stood under my oriental persimmon tree. I touched the wrinkled bark surface, as the tree moved in the wind, its branches waving outward in ever-widening circles, circles confluent with one another, each influencing another's outcome.

I turned back toward the future doctor.

"It's been a number of years now, Rick. I'm sure the good professor has engaged in many a discussion with the original author of Ecclesiastes.

"You know, I have always marveled at the interaction of events—how a single happening occurs at the same time as others, and together they become a unified wave that rolls over us."

"That's a bit too deep for me, Doc."

"Me, too, Rick, but I can never erase some memories..."

December was warm that fateful, long-ago year.

"Bob, baby Seth passed away this morning."

It was Tom Paulson.

"Thanks for letting me know."

He had called at 5:30 a.m. Now it was noon.

"Dr. Galen, the Daumier boy is here—says he wants to give you something."

I got up and walked out to the waiting room.

"Doc, here's an invite."

Alex had turned fifteen. He was taller now. He handed me a hand-printed card: YOU ARE INVITED TO MY EAGLE SCOUT CEREMONY

I shook his hand.

"I'll try to get there, Alex."

"Don't just try, Doc. Be there!"

He flashed a grin and left.

6:30 p.m.

"Dr. Galen, a call for you."

It was Tom Regelson's wife, Kim. She had remained night and day by her husband's bedside in the hospital's hospice wing. I made a point of visiting him as often as I could. Her call caught me just as I was about to head over there.

I knocked gently on the closed door of room 903. Kim opened it. She was exhausted.

"He's had a bad day. I don't know what to do, Dr. Galen."

"Go get some rest. I'll stay with him for a while. Go lie down, Kim."

She left. I sat down in the yellow, vinyl-covered chair next to Tom's bed. He had slipped into a coma before I arrived. Pictures of his family—sons, daughter, wife—were positioned on the table at the foot of the bed. Older pictures of his parents and siblings lay propped up on another bedside table. On the opposite wall were some paintings he had done, scenes of his boyhood in Minnesota.

Something else caught my eye. It was a small, maple, wall plaque that had been stained a cherry-dark maroon.

Its letters had been incused with a burning tool. It was the Boy Scout Oath, dated almost seventy years before. At the bottom, scrawled in a childish hand: TOMMY REGELSON.

Kim came back an hour later. We sat there, until he died at 8:50 p.m.

I asked her if I could have the plaque, and she gave it to me.

The following Saturday, I gave it to Alex Daumier at his Eagle Scout ceremony.

Hey Rube!

The woman's voice was barely audible.

"This is Beatrice Gordon. My sister Samantha and I live with Maude and..."

I interrupted her.

"What can I do for you, Miss Gordon?"

I was not a patient man in my younger days.

"Could you come by the house?"

"Now?"

That Halloween night the temperature had dropped into the high twenties, and the wind gusts gave only a taste of the winter yet to come. Most of the neighborhood parents had kept all but the oldest kids indoors, so the usual parade of trick-or-treaters had withered to an occasional junior high-schooler, something that truly upset my beloved Cathy. She loved to see the costumed munchkins showing up at our door.

I tried my best to suggest to Beatrice that morning would be better.

"Are you sure this can't wait until morning, Miss Gordon?"

She had called at 11:45 p.m.

"Yes, Dr. Galen."

"Why?"

"Maude's feeling poorly."

I sighed, hung up, and put on my outside clothes.

"Do you have to go out tonight, Tony?"

Cathy was sitting in bed reading.

"'Fraid so. Maude needs me."

"You got a new girlfriend?"

"Nope, can't handle the one I got now."

I bent over and kissed her, grabbed my black bag, and headed out to the car.

Maude Gordon, nice little old lady—lol to you savvy medical types—had been one of my very first patients the year I opened my home office. And, like all my other early patients, she had walked in unannounced.

"Is this really a doctor's office?"

The air conditioning had been working overtime to repel the heat and cloying humidity so typical of a Northern Virginia summer. The previous week's rains had given birth to a bumper crop of mosquitoes as well.

I had worked day and night to get the office ready for its grand opening on the first of July. The smell of fresh paint hung in the air, as I called out a response.

"Yes, ma'am, what can we do for you?"

"Are you the doctor?"

"Yes, I am."

I wasn't wearing the prerequisite white coat and tie considered de rigueur for doctors back then. I never did like them—still don't—but I must admit that my Hawaiian short-sleeve shirt and khaki pants disconcerted the prim, elderly woman.

"Can you see me? I seem to be having a problem with my skin, and my regular doctor is on vacation."

Young doctors better get used to hearing the expression "regular doctor." I always wondered if that meant I was irregular, maybe having a bowel dysfunction that attracted patients who couldn't see their own normally bowelled physicians.

"Please come in, Miss..."

"I'm Maude Gordon."

She was one of those diminutive women who turned heads in their younger days and still possessed an indefinable something that spoke quality. Silver-gray hair flowed above a faultless, clear-skinned face with sapphire-blue eyes. No makeup—none needed—even in what I presumed to be her early seventies.

The simple, white, long-sleeved blouse and light-tan skirt showed a well-kept figure, with thin-but-muscular calves that reminded me of a professional ballerina.

"What seems to be the problem, Miss Gordon?"

"My back and left arm feel like they're on fire, and now these welts just appeared."

I held my breath. I was hoping it wouldn't be what I suspected.

She unbuttoned the sleeve on her blouse, and the diagnosis was obvious: shingles. Herpes zoster—adult chickenpox.

Back in those primitive days we didn't have anything to treat it except pain medication, topical lotions, and an anti-seizure drug called Dilantin to try to block the nerve pain.

Imagine a hot poker touching your skin that no one can take away. The burning, shooting pain runs a course from back to front along a highway of nerve fibers. That's what shingles can feel like.

"Miss Gordon, I'm sorry to say you have shingles."

Before I could continue, the old woman interrupted.

"Don't be silly, young man. My house has a slate roof."

Uh-oh. I started to wonder if Maude Gordon was dealing with a full deck.

Then she laughed, as my face gave my thoughts away.

"No, young man, I'm not nuts—I just couldn't resist saying that."

She giggled like a school girl and gave me a coquettish look.

"I'm sorry. I owe you an explanation, too. But tell me, what can I do for this ... this stuff on my arm?"

I waved my magic doctor rattle, told her about the lotions and pills, and warned her there really was nothing medically I could do.

That was then. Today I can whip out a prescription for drugs that will stop the virus in its tracks or even give a geriatric patient a vaccination to prevent it.

But Miss Maude seemed so understanding, even downright stoic, about the prospect of post-herpetic neuralgia—the lingering, persistent pain.

"Now, Doctor, would you like to take my history, such as it is?"

I did. There was something very compelling about the woman. She seemed uniquely young for her age, yet she showed signs of an ancient wisdom—I just couldn't put my finger on it.

I grabbed one of my brand-new, freshly printed, medical-history data sheets and placed it in a clipboard. I snatched a pen and sat down across the examining table from her.

"Miss Gordon, let me get your full name and address first."

Maude Mehitibel Gordon. She didn't live that far away: four blocks and turn right at the first light, then four blocks more.

"Your birthday?"

"Doctor, don't you know that a gentleman never asks a lady her age?"

"Yes, ma'am, I do, but unfortunately I need to ask."

She gave me a birthdate from the time of William McKinley.

"What type of work did you do?"

I assumed she was a retired teacher or government worker. She beamed at me. I could have sworn she was a part of some cosmic joke.

"Well, young man, my two sisters, Samantha, Beatrice, and I were barnstormers and dinger girls. We had one heck of a G-bit, too."

Her look just dared me to ask what the hell she was talking about.

Holy smoke! She was a carny!

Now it was my turn. I gave her my best, enigmatic, male version of a Mona Lisa smile and fake Virginia accent.

"Well, Miss Gordon, if that just don't beat all. When I was a kid I was a gazoonie!"

"Berto, Berto, come on, the circus is in town!"

Sal, my one surviving neighborhood friend, flexed his muscle-bound body and shifted impatiently from one foot to the next, as he waited on the stoop outside my tenement.

I was almost seventeen and feeling oats I never knew I had. It was a beautiful Saturday in early May, and I had been going stir crazy after almost a week of dismal, rainy weather. I had finished my homework and there were no chores to do.

"Mama, I'm going out."

Yes, I was past the age of asking permission, but the unspoken "please, may I?" was always there, and she knew it.

Si, Berto."

Then she stuck her head out the front window and yelled down at Sal.

"You two stay away from the girls. *Capisch,* Salvatore Gatto?"

Sal looked up and flashed one of his famous smiles that could make girls of all ages swoon.

"Si, Signora Galen, but remember I'm just a big alley cat!"

I stuck my head out the window.

"Don't you mean Sally cat?"

Mama and I both laughed. I blew her a kiss and headed out the door.

Sal was just a few days older than I, and by then we were both studs on the prowl. What better place to see pretty girls than the circus that had just put down its tent stakes on the outskirts of Newark.

No, it wasn't Ringling Brothers or Barnum and Bailey (back then they were still separate organizations). The big circuses always wound up at Madison Square Garden in Manhattan. This was one of those traveling carnivals featuring either not-ready-for-primetime or well-ripened performers—a few scraggly, geriatric animals, overweight tightrope walkers, clumsy clowns—plus lots of grifters and games on the midway.

The carnivals followed well-established travel routes, starting out in Florida or the Gulf Coast and moving north as the weather warmed. This particular enterprise had set up on a vacant property near the swamps and pig farms that sat between Newark and New York.

We didn't have bus fare, so we walked for forty-five minutes, the two of us exchanging raucous and lewd comments about what we would see and do once we got there.

Suddenly I stopped in realization.

"Sal, these things cost money. How're we gonna get in?"

We were too big and cool to scrounge for soda-pop bottles. We left that to the little kids now, although sometimes, when I was alone and it was getting dark, I would still pick up a few.

Once more he flashed that Cheshire grin then poked my shoulder.

"Come on, Mr. Muscles, we're gonna be roustabouts. They'll let us in for free."

I should have known. With Sal, fun always came with a catch. This time I'd be huffing and puffing, while Mr. Hercules Gatto would breeze through whatever labors our adventure required.

We could hear it all from blocks away: the calliope music, accompanied by shouts of "try your luck," the trumpets and drums of the band, the pop-pop-pop of the shooting galleries, and the din of the crowd. The air hung heavy with the aromas of spun sugar and popcorn, with vague hints of hotdogs and mustard, and a tinge of pig farm and swamp thrown in for good measure.

The guy at the gate looked us up and down, as if he knew instinctively we weren't cash customers.

Sal just grinned at him.

"Need any work done, mistah?"

He flexed his muscles and the guy's eyes lit up. Then the one-headed, human Cerberus turned his gaze on me. I didn't have anything to flex. But he let us in anyway. I guess he figured he'd get twice the work out of Sal.

"Yeah, kid, see that guy over there? That's Fred. Tell him I sent the two of you over. He'll give ya yer ducats."

Then, as an afterthought, he yelled out, "Hey, Fred, we got us a coupla gazoonies!"

Neither one of us knew what the hell the guy was talking about. We just knew we were in.

A half-hour later, after mucking out the ammonia-tinged, urine-soaked sawdust from the areas where two, moribund, old lions hung out, I figured out a rough translation of gazoonies: young suckers.

Before old Fred handed us our ducats—actually free passes—he took a moment to look us over. Then he winked at Sal.

"You young bucks oughta go see the girlie show."

Naturally that's where Sal dragged me, after we hosed the big-cat urine stink off each other. But we had to pass a number of concessions on the way, and I slowed him and his libido down by stopping, pointing, and looking at the different displays. We saw shooting galleries with both live-ammunition and photoelectric-cell mechanical bears, ducks, Hitlers, and Tojos that would jump and scream if the light from your gun triggered the cell. And there were cotton-candy stands surrounded by sticky-faced little urchins smearing the stuff on their clothes and then demanding more.

What really caught my eye was a guy with a little blowtorch who heated and twisted glass rods of all sizes into toy animals. But Sal just yawned and kept pulling at me—until he saw a guy holding a big, wooden hammer and standing in front of a tower, daring one and all to show their lady friends how strong they really were.

"Hit the peg and ring the bell and win a prize for your lady love!"

I spotted a dime on the sawdust-covered dirt, snatched it up before a little kid was about to lunge for it, and handed it to Sal.

"Here, Nature Boy, strut your stuff."

"You ain't my lady love, Berto."

"You bet your sweet ass I'm not, muscle brain. Too scared to try it?"

He flipped the dime at the concessionaire—a Mercury head if I recall correctly—and grabbed the hammer from the man's hand. After giving me the finger he raised the hammer high and slammed it as hard as he could on the fulcrum.

Damn if the sliding weight didn't rise to the top of the tower and hit the bell—"bong!" The crowd clapped and whistled, and Sal turned to face them. He made his right bicep muscle pop up and strutted away.

"Hey, kid, don'cher want yer prize?"

Sal turned back and took the stuffed bear, held it up to more applause, and threw it at me. The crowd guffawed; I held it to my face and kissed it.

"Come on, gentlemen, ya gonna let that kid beat ya? Show him yer moxie. C'mon, take a turn, just ten cents, one thin dime!"

We moved on toward the girlie show. I saw a little girl standing next to her mother. I walked over and handed the kid the bear. I figure today I'd probably be arrested for such effrontery. But back then the mother just smiled and thanked me.

We passed more food and game stands, and then we saw the freak-show tents: the Bearded Lady, the Lizard Man, the Human Pretzel, the Indian Mystic.

Suddenly Sal jumped and pointed at the barker standing outside and hawking away.

"Girls, count 'em fellas, girls who know the secret dances of the Orient! Step right up! Step right up!"

Sal flashed our ducats, and the barker waved us through. He smiled, which I now know implied "here's two more Johns." Back then I was clueless.

The tent was poorly lit and stunk of cigar smoke, cheap booze, unwashed bodies, and lust. The barker joined the party, after everyone had plopped down on hard, open-backed, wooden benches. The place was full of horny guys ranging in age from teens like us to white-haired lechers.

"Gentlemen, you are going to see the most amazing demonstration of Terpsichore since Cleopatra wooed Caesar, since Madame Bovary voulez-voused with the king of France. I give you The Fantastic Francine and her sisters Fiona and Fannie!"

At that, three, let's call them Rubenesque ladies—who probably had celebrated their thirtieth birthdays well more than a decade before—came bouncing out, kicking up their legs in a feeble imitation of the Radio City Rockettes. That lasted for about two minutes. Then they turned around, bent over, and flipped their threadbare costumes above their backsides.

The barker stood up, climbed on stage, and winked.

"Gentlemen, now our ladies will put on some special performances that will engage your ... minds! For just two bits, gentlemen—twenty-five cents! And, gentlemen, let me tell you, Francine and her sisters are the finest G-bit dancers in the world!"

That was the pitch. The girls were dingers—they started with a chorus-line dance to hook the audience, and then the barker would do a bait-and-switch to prod more money out of the eager, pliable males. The unspoken promise, hinted at by the expression "G-bit," was a full strip-tease.

Sal was all for it. He waved our ducats at the barker, but the pitchman shook his head.

"Not for this stuff, guys."

Sal was not one to take no for an answer. He grabbed the front of the little man's shirt.

It was almost as if Sal had inadvertently pushed a hidden button.

"Hey, Rube!"

That barker had one helluva voice.

Sal and I took off at a run, and the rest of the audience wasn't far behind.

We made it to the corner of another tent and peered around the edge. About twenty carnies—carnival employees—converged on the girlie-show tent. We could hear loud voices and cries of "get those gazoonies!"

We managed to sneak away and ran most of the way home.

Sal needed to use the bathroom by the time we got to my place, so I waved him up the stairs behind me. We walked in and my mother's nose immediately wrinkled in disgust. She looked at us and uttered one word: "Miao!"

Our hosing off didn't quite remove the *eau de lion* scent.

Mama ordered us to wash up, "pronto." I lent Sal a pair of pants and a shirt that barely fit him, and then he headed home.

As I recounted my one-day carny job to Maude Gordon, she kept clapping her hands in delight with each twist and turn. When I mentioned Francine, she exclaimed, "Oh, my goodness, young man, I knew those girls. They started up just about the time my sisters and I hung up our G-strings.

"Poor Francine, I heard she had her neck snapped by a john in Alabama. Fannie and Fiona married other carnies. I think they're living down near Carny Town now."

She was referring to Gibsonton, Florida.

After that, Maude never returned to her regular doctor. She would always show up, unannounced, and I would see her and let her regale me with tales of the carny life.

When she learned of my interest in aviation she described her barnstorming years right after World War I, doing a wing-walker routine with her sisters in a fragile, cloth-and-balsa-wood, single-engine biplane that "was held together by spit and bailing wire."

It was flown by her boyfriend, an ex-pilot doughboy. They had planned to marry, but he crashed in a solo routine that required him to fly through open barn doors during a gig in Kansas. The prairie wind had swung the back pair of doors closed just as he flew in.

During the roaring twenties, Maude and her sisters, Iowa farm girls all, switched to the carny life.

"In a way, we were lucky," she told me. "When the Depression hit the country, at least we had a carny wagon to live in."

I asked her why she and her sisters didn't stay in Iowa."

"Didn't you ever want to run away from home, Doctor?"

I told her about how I once met an old 'bo—a hobo—in the Newark railroad yards, and how he had talked me out of it.

She smiled.

"Ever been to Iowa? We were wild, Doctor. Iowa was the end of the world back then. When Mr. (President Woodrow) Wilson sent the boys 'over there,' my sisters and I volunteered to serve as nurses' helpers. And, as the saying goes, how ya gonna keep 'em down on the farm, after they've seen Paree?"

I thought of the three Old Guys back in the tenements, and I understood.

Maude remained my patient over the next fifteen years, and some of her stories I cannot repeat in polite company.

She showed me how she had learned to lift wallets in a magic-show act and how to yell "Hey, Rube!" at the top of her lungs, if any of the clientele became what the carnies called "rough trade."

And then, the Halloween-night phone call from her sisters summoned me.

I pulled up to the Victorian-style, two-story house and had to use a pocket flashlight to find my way up the porch steps. I knocked, and the front door, unlatched, swung open.

The house was cold, and the hallway was empty. I called out a "hello," and a tiny voice replied from the front parlor.

"In here, Doctor."

Light from a 15-watt bulb barely illuminated an old sofa and the two, fragile-looking ladies sitting there.

I kept my coat on.

"Hello Miss Samantha, Miss Beatrice. Where's Maude?"

"She's upstairs, Dr. Galen."

"Yes, she's upstairs, Doctor."

"Did she tell you what's bothering her?"

"She said she's feeling poorly."

I climbed the stairs in the dark, holding tightly to the loose handrailing to avoid tripping over the warped steps. Another dim light shone from the first room at the top. I entered.

"Hello Maude."

No answer.

I moved closer to the bed and touched the hand sticking out from under the bed sheet. It was cold—no more than room temperature. I took my stethoscope out of my bag and listened: no breath sounds or heart beats. I pulled up half-closed eyelids. Her pupils were fixed in center position and dilated. And I could smell the mixed scent of loosened bowel and bladder.

I walked slowly back down the stairs and reentered the parlor.

"When was the last time you ladies spoke with Maude?"

"Just before you arrived, Doctor."

"Yes, just before you arrived."

"Did she say anything?"

"Oh, yes, Doctor. She asked us to call you."

From what I had seen, Maude had been dead for at least six hours.

"I'm afraid I have some bad news, ladies. Your sister has folded her tent."

The two women turned to each other then smiled at me.

"Thank you for coming, Doctor."

"Uh ... would you like me to call the funeral home?"

"That would be nice, Doctor."

"Yes, Doctor, that would be nice."

They pointed to an old, candle-stick-style phone on an end table. I went to it and dialed the mortician's number.

After fifteen years in practice I knew it by heart.

I stayed with Maude's sisters until the mortuary car, a converted Chevy van, arrived. Soon two men walked in with a folded, go-to-Jesus cart. I pointed to the stairs, and the lead man nodded.

Several minutes later, I heard them coming down slowly, this time the cart wheels and table support fully extended. On it was the familiar, rubber body bag, now filled and zipped up.

Maude's sisters rose and went into the hallway.

"Can we say goodbye?"

I nodded, and the mortuary men unzipped the top of the bag. Maude's face was framed in the opening. The two women came forward and touched her forehead.

"Break a leg, Maude."

"Yes, Maudie, break a leg."

The lead man re-zipped the bag.

I made up the rear of the procession out the front door and down the steps. The mortician turned to me, after his men lifted the cart into the van.

"We'll bring the death certificate by your office, Doc."

"Thanks, Henry."

"Uh ... Doc ... ya want us to take the other two?"

"Henry, they're still alive."

"Are ya sure, Doc?"

I got back in my car and drove home. It was 1:30 a.m. on the first of November.

I slipped into pajamas and climbed in bed next to Cathy.

I didn't wake her.

The Dork

Common sense is a most uncommon commodity.

—Ramesh Bhatia

"I look like a dork!"

The kid was right.

Picture a fifteen-year-old male, reed-thin, with a chicken-beak nose and an Adam's apple that would choke a horse. Add one, pre-pubertal, hatchet-shaped face capped by cow-licked, red hair, then set the whole head on a scrawny neck. At five-feet-two inches, 80 pounds, and arms much too long for his torso, he looked like an emaciated orangutan.

And since you asked, he wore eyeglasses, dental braces, and his feet were disproportionately large.

Voila! Dork.

Nate Criswell sat apart from his parents, Dell and Marlene Criswell, who had brought the boy in for a routine checkup. What evolved was a list of worries on their part and misery on his.

Why was he so thin?

Why hadn't he hit puberty yet?

Why was he…?

I reviewed his health records: normal delivery; two older siblings, both very tall, and no unusual childhood diseases or injuries. His parents' health histories likewise were unremarkable.

"Nate, you aren't by any chance from New Jersey, are you?"

"Yeah, why?"

"It's been a long time since I heard anyone say 'dork.'"

I stared at the awkward kid and remembered someone from my old neighborhood: Paolo Cherubini. The last I had heard, that FLK (funny looking kid) had grown up to own a chain of boutique, watch-and-clock shops.

"Nothing really, it's just a Jersey thing, right?"

There, a slight smile.

"Let's take a look at you, Nate. Do you want your folks in here with you?"

"No way!"

I shooed them out of the room.

I took his vital signs and told him to remove his shirt. His chest fit the chicken motif—*pectus carina*—an outbowing of the rib cage like a bird's breast. That didn't necessarily mean anything bad. And his father appeared to have the same build.

"Doc, why do I look this way?"

"Nate, don't sweat it. You should have seen what I looked like at your age."

I didn't have the heart to tell him that I at least looked human. I sometimes lie to avoid hurting a patient's sensitive feelings.

"Nate, first of all, it's genetics. You resemble your dad at lot. He's not a bad-looking guy. I'll bet if I saw a photo of him as a kid, I'd think it was you."

As I said, I lie easily.

"But all my friends are..."

I cut him short.

"They're all following their parents' genetic blueprints."

"What's a blueprint?"

"It's like programming."

He understood that one.

"I have a feeling you're going to start growing a lot this year."

Now I wasn't lying. We determine the pubertal (physical and sexual) development of kids with a descriptive scale called Tanner Stages. Physically, Nate's body was leaving the pre-adolescent Stage 0 and was showing some of the changes expected for Stage I. Once that starts, it's Katy, bar the door. Your nice quiet kid becomes a surly, mall-stalking nocturnal monster.

The rest of my examination confirmed that suspicion. Nate was right on the verge of joining the human race.

I noticed something else about him: As he was being examined, he asked a lot of questions.

"Why do you shine that light at my eyes?"

"What do you hear in my chest?"

He wanted to know about the gadgets I used and the maneuvers I put him through. He wanted to hold the toys I played with—to try them out, to know what they did.

After I finished, he got dressed, and I looked him in the eye.

"Nate, you're normal."

I sat down with his parents and went over my findings. Then I turned to Nate and gave him my usual, sympathetic advice:

"Kwitcherbellyachin', kid. Things are gonna get better."

The three smiled, as they left the office.

Two years later I was looking up at a six-foot-two-inch, one-hundred-fifty-pound teenager, complete with zits and raging hormones.

Nate had revealed an aptitude for science. It was not unusual to find him sitting in my waiting room after school with a list of questions about chemistry, biology—and girls. He also hung around and, if I had something interesting going on, he would ask me and the patient if he could sit in on the examination.

Corrado, my mentor, I think we've got another disciple of Aesclepius.

By the time he graduated from high school, I knew what Nate's career goal would be. I was the first to learn of his intent to take science majors in college and then try out for a place in medical school.

Life wasn't easy for that tall young man. His face still looked dorky, he was awkward at socialization, and coeds remained an arcane mystery—but classes were a breeze.

The same year his braces finally came off, I suggested contact lenses. It helped make him look less geeky. Then, after much verbal struggle, he finally got rid of the suspenders and wore a belt. The only thing I couldn't persuade him to do was undergo cosmetic surgery for his beak nose.

So, what finally got the girls to notice him without laughing?

It turned out Nate was an artist. Give him a piece of wood and, as Michelangelo once said, he would release the sculpture within. Watercolors, oils, and acrylics were an outlet to his mind's eye. Give him a part, a brief image, and he could envision the whole.

And when he lacked the right tools, he would invent new ones.

"Doc, I got accepted!"

It was March of his senior year at university. He had done well academically and, like his puberty, dating arrived later than normal—but better later than never.

Now Nate was ready to take on med school.

He would call me late at night on a weekly—sometimes daily—basis.

"We named our cadaver George."

And…

"They had this one specimen in pathology that…"

And…

"I start on the wards tomorrow."

And…

"Doc, my patient died…"

And finally…

"You should have seen the case I had to work up today, Doc. Bet you can't guess what the diagnosis is!"

He launched into a long description of a young woman with unusual abdominal pain in the middle of her second trimester (fourth to sixth months) of her pregnancy.

I hated to do it, really I did.

"Nate, she's got an atypical presentation of appendicitis."

"Damn, how'd you do that, Doc?"

"Elementary, my dear Watson."

Heh, heh, I lied again—I really enjoyed doing that!

I attended Nate's graduation. He actually looked good in his doctoral gown and green-and-gold hood. As he walked up on stage, I remembered another class, another time, when my friends and I did the same.

He grinned at me, as he walked by me in the recessional. And when he passed, he gave me a thumbs-up.

"Well, Nate, still think you're a dork?"

We were standing outside the auditorium. A girl stood next to him. She looked up at his hatchet face.

"What's a dork, Nate?"

He blushed.

I took a piece of paper and printed out:

D~~O~~R~~K~~

I shook his hand.

"Congratulations, Dr. Criswell."

The Garden

"You've got a good-looking colon, Dr. Galen."

I would have preferred, "hey, good lookin'," but I had just awakened from the anesthesia used for my routine colonoscopy, so I took the comment as a compliment.

I lay there dressed in a gown, hat, and support stockings, an outfit that made me the spitting image of J. Edgar Hoover, pre-drag.

I stared up at the young nurse who was removing the IV needle from my hand and belched out a "thanks."

They do use a helluva lot of air in a colonoscopy.

Please, no jokes.

Getting dressed restored a modicum of my dignity, but it promptly disappeared, as they required me to sit in a wheelchair and be pushed out to the car, where my designated driver waited to take me home.

It was a short ride back, but I remained silent. Even a normal colonoscopy was nothing to sneeze at, especially at my age. Yet it was always something to be desired. Why couldn't that have been "St. Nick's" diagnosis?

Charlie Willard. Santa Claus.

It was one of those mid-spring Sundays in northern Virginia, when the weather was faultless. A Mediterranean-blue sky lit by a golden sun rested lightly on the natural air-conditioning provided by a light breeze. Dressed in my old scrub shirt and pants, I was trying to hand-turn an eight-by-eight-foot section of clay and rock out in the yard. I had hoped to grow tomatoes. It was my first real home—a little house with grassy yard—and I actually believed the plant-catalogue photos of bountiful harvests with little or no work involved.

Uh-huh. The blisters rising on my palms belied that prospect.

I didn't hear the car pull in behind me, but I did hear a deep voice bellow, "My wife just cut her finger fixing dinner, Doc. Can you sew it up?"

My face was covered with sweat and grime, when I turned to see the living personification of Thomas Nast's Santa Claus protectively holding his wife's hand like a pet dog's injured paw. I didn't say a word—I felt a little ticked off at being disturbed in my garden reverie. So, I just nodded my head, waved my arm in a "follow-me" motion, and headed inside.

I carefully scrubbed the dirt off my hands, cleansed and prepared the woman's skin, and proceeded to numb up and suture the wound.

Each and every time I attended to this basic medical chore, my mind brought me back to that first equivalent of a house call, when I cut my proverbial medical teeth as a kid by sewing up a wounded gang member, a feat that had earned me the nickname *Dottore* Berto.

While I sat there, gloved and masked, Santa introduced himself.

"Doc, I'm Charlie Willard. This is my wife, Sarah. We saw your sign go up a few months ago, and since we live just down the street from you ... oh, hell, I didn't want my Sarah to have to sit in some damned emergency room!"

I laughed through the mask.

"Yeah, I can understand that, Mr. Willard. I've been the guy in the ER having to see folks like you in between auto accidents and other goodies."

His deep laugh only needed a "ho-ho-ho" to complete the picture.

Sarah Willard, sitting across from me, with her arm lying on the exam table, added just the right touch.

"Oh, hush up, Charlie. He's just a big baby, Dr. Galen. I thought he was going to pass out, when he saw the blood on my finger."

The big guy blushed. He shot a look of embarrassment at the round-faced, white-haired woman who had shared his life for three decades. They were truly Mr. and Mrs. Claus in the flesh.

Charlie had just retired from over thirty years' service at an unnamed government agency. He proudly boasted of his grown children and their accomplishments, and he winked at me knowingly, when he mentioned a new generation was on the way. Clearly he had put the stresses of his career behind him.

I finished suturing and dressing Sarah's hand and administered a tetanus shot in her left shoulder. As they headed past me toward the door, Charlie turned and patted me on the shoulder.

"Go rest up, Doc. I'll finish for you."

And finish he did! Twenty minutes later he returned, driving a little pickup truck. Shortly thereafter I heard the "brapp-brapp" of a power tiller starting up. Charlie handled it like a bucking bronco, as it broke up the ground's rock-hard, red clay into soft clods.

His six-foot-two-inch, three-hundred-pound frame hefted a four-foot bale of peat moss and four bags of composted cow manure off the truck's bed like bags of feathers. He tossed them onto the now-turned ground, bent over, split the bags open with his combination bottle opener/pen knife, and spread them over the patch of earth. Then he drove the bucking-bronco tiller again, until the plant-savers were thoroughly mixed into beautiful, dark-brown soil.

The tomatoes that erupted from my little garden later that summer were the best I had ever tasted.

Several years passed. Charlie and Sarah became routine visitors to my office. So did their kids, who soon enough had kids of their own. I saw them all. And every spring, like clockwork, Charlie would show up with his tiller to mix more goodies into the soil. My backyard garden produced harvest after harvest, as did Charlie and Sarah's children.

Then one morning Charlie dropped by unannounced. I could see his red-faced embarrassment, as he blurted out, "I noticed some blood in the toilet bowl this morning, Doc."

I didn't want to wait until he had done a bowel cleansing. I had him lie down on the examining table, while I pulled out one of those primitive torture devices we used back then: an eighteen-inch, metal proctoscope. Solid chrome steel and totally inflexible, the Silver Stallion, as it was nicknamed, was considered state-of-the-art before the days of fiber optics. Patients dreaded it. They didn't appreciate the sensation it produced, as it threaded its way up their lower intestines.

I pumped air into the scope to inflate and push the bowel walls away from its tip.

"Oh, hell."

I couldn't control the expletive, and Charlie Willard heard me.

"What is it, Doc?"

The blood-red living devil stared back at me from inside Charlie's bowel.

Santa Claus had colon cancer.

The surgeon did a masterful job removing fourteen inches of Charlie's colon. He gave me a thumbs-up and a muffled, "We got the bastard out," from behind his mask then exited the OR.

We all thought that the tumor had been found early, but the Fates weren't going to let Charlie Willard off that easy.

Several months after the surgery, I spotted the insidious enlargement of Charlie's liver. Despite attempts at chemotherapy, he began the inevitable wasting process of uncontrolled, widespread, metastatic cancer.

An old man wonders: With the imaging technology and targeted chemotherapy we have available today, would things have gone differently?

It was late spring of the following year, and I was outside playing in my vegetable patch once more. But Charlie didn't appear to perform his tilling; the cancer had weakened him too much.

By then I could turn over the ground by hand without suffering blisters. Charlie's labors had transformed the soil into loose, moist clods. My shovel easily sank twelve inches into the grave-dark depths, as I prepared holes for the tomato plants.

Then, out of the corner of my eye I spotted movement. I turned to see Charlie standing there patiently watching me.

Suddenly I felt puzzled: Charlie had terminal colon cancer. I had seen him at home earlier in the week. He wasn't doing well. My anger and frustration at not being able to restore this man to health had made me somewhat testy.

"Charlie, what the hell are you doing out here? It's too hot for you."

His jowly face, thinner now, still broke a grin.

"Just taking care of some unfinished business, Doc."

I settled down.

"Charlie, do you want me to drive you home?"

He shook his head.

"Okay, why don't you head back, and I'll stop by after I clean up. Let Sarah know I'll be coming over."

"Okay, Doc."

I turned away to drop the last tomato plant into its hole. I turned back and Charlie was gone.

I finally got all the plants in the way I wanted. Then I washed up, changed into my khaki walking trousers, and headed down the block, my black bag making a pendulum bob of my right hand.

Charlie's house was an oyster-white Cape Cod with green shutters framing the windows. I rang the doorbell, and Sarah opened the white-paneled front door. Her ashen face revealed that something was not right.

I stood there somewhat sheepishly.

"Hello, Sarah. Charlie stopped by my place earlier, and I told him I'd come by after I finished planting."

She stared at me then silently pointed to the stairs leading up to their bedroom.

I climbed up the eleven steps before entering the tan-carpeted room. A poster-style, king-size bed sat in the middle. The western-sky sun was casting light and shadow through the two windows on the far wall.

Charlie, in light-brown pajamas, lay propped up on pillows. His skin was jaundiced, and his eyes were filmy and sunken. His chest was rising and falling in shallow motions.

As I approached his bed, his mouth opened, fish-wide, in a futile last gasp. Slowly a stain spread across his pajama pants, as his bladder sphincter failed. He died in front of me.

A tearful voice behind me whispered, "He hasn't left this room the entire week."

I turned and held his widow.

An Eagle Flew West

The old farmhouse was gone.

So, too, were the unpaved, dirt roads and much of the wooded areas in the little enclave just west of Lynchburg.

Big Dave and Mary were gone, too.

But I remembered.

Hey, City Boy, why don't you just roll around in the cow patties? You'll get less of it on you than you're picking up now.

I heard the familiar, nasal drawl once more, but only in my mind.

Country Boy was gone.

The woods were still there, or maybe they were the descendants of the trees and scrub underbrush, where Dave and I had walked over forty years before. I could see houses through the leafless branches on that cold November day. The tobacco fields were now five- and ten-acre spreads of enormous homes filled with city folk who had sought the dream of country living. Now their lifestyle polluted the former open spaces.

I walked through the woods again that day.

I got lost at first and wandered around until the wind told me, *That way, City Boy.*

I entered the little clearing. The peaks and valleys were not as prominent—over four decades of seasonal changes can do that to overturned soil, but two were still fairly fresh. I stood there, eyes closed, head bent, remembering the old folks who had treated me as a second son, who had laughed at my city ways and then consoled me and taught me what life could offer.

I felt the chill in my bones. Two-score-plus years can do that, too, but I removed my gloves and reached into an inner pocket of my heavy, gray-knit coat. The small, glass container, given to me by the funeral director in Florida, was still in there, still holding some of the gray-white powder that had once been the man who walked here with me, loved a wife, and raised two children.

I opened it and held it up to the sky. A gust of wind coursed through the naked trees, and the dust that had once been my friend joined that of his ancestors.

It was too late to drive back to Northern Virginia. Once I would have done so without hesitation. Now I feared the limitations of mind and body that had been imposed upon me. Truth be told, I no longer enjoyed driving, especially at night, and the November sunlight would soon vanish.

So I placed the empty vial between the two mounds and cast one final gaze at my past.

I would never return here.

I drove down the highway a few miles and spotted a roadside motel. This time of year vacancies were not a problem. The graveled parking lot was empty.

Minutes later, key in hand, I walked out of the office and down the row of closed doors to my room.

I wasn't hungry. I lay down on the little bed and closed my eyes. I felt at ease, so I drifted into slumber.

But it wouldn't last long.

I awoke to a sudden, loud scream and a shout.

"Easy, honey, easy, I'll call the ambulance. Just hang on!"

I heard the young man's panicky voice and the woman's crescendo moans, and her stifled screams penetrating the wall of the room next to mine. They must have checked in after I arrived.

I got up, smoothed my wrinkled clothes, and grabbed my black bag, which I always carried on my travels, even in the twilight of my career.

The door of the next room lay partly open. I raised my hand and knocked. I called through the opening, "May I come in?"

I saw the young woman lying on the bed, her knees drawn up, her belly a watermelon mound under the sheets. She was pregnant, very pregnant.

"Are you the doctor?"

"I'm a doctor, yes, ma'am."

She was gasping between the contractions, which were only seconds apart. Things were going to happen very soon.

I rolled up my sleeves, quickly washed my hands, and found a pack of disposable, sterile gloves in my bag. It had been a long time since I had delivered a baby.

"Easy now, take slow breaths. Easy, easy..."

As I said, it had been a while, but I couldn't forget. My reflexes have grown slower, my eyesight not as keen, but I still knew. I saw the cervix one-hundred-percent dilated. I saw the baby's head.

Thank God it was a vertex (head) presentation.

I reached in using two fingers of my left hand to guide the baby's head down and to the left, as my right hand eased first one shoulder and then the next through that life portal. My efforts were rewarded with a loud, red-faced squall.

It was a boy.

I had set two hemostats (clamps) on paper towels, and now I used them to clamp off the umbilical cord. Once more my bag brought forth what I needed—scissors—and I cut the cord between the clamps. Then I applied gentle pressure to the young woman's abdomen, and the placenta—that amazing organ joining the baby to its mother that is the baby's lifeline—eased out of the uterus.

I wrapped the newborn in an extra sheet and held it. I looked at the woman, now forever Mama, Mommy—Mother!

"What's your son's name?"

She was tired.

"We haven't decided yet."

She looked at me.

"Is the ambulance outside?"

"Not yet."

"Then how did you…"

"I was in the room next door."

I handed the baby to her, and she held it against her breast, as I sat, exhausted.

"What's your name?"

She smiled at me.

"Galen. Robert Galen. And yours?"

"Tammy Santos. We were heading south to Florida for work, and then my water broke. How did you get here?"

I told her of my trip to Florida for my friend's funeral and eulogy. I told her how he and I had once roamed the farmland that had defined this area so many years ago. And I told her of my visit to his family plot.

"What was his name?"

She was getting sleepy now, but I told her.

The ambulance siren startled us both.

The door flew open, and a crew of EMTs rushed in, followed by a haggard young man calling out, "Tammy, Tammy, are you all right?"

One of the techs looked at me and saw my bag on the side table.

"You a doc, old timer?"

"Yeah, young fella—and I'm not so old yet. Better check the baby's blood sugar. Get him warmed up, and get him and his mama to the hospital. Oh, I saved the placenta. Be sure to give it to the hospital, too. His time of birth was 6:50 a.m.

"How's that sound to you, youngster?"

"You still got it, Doc!"

"Damn straight!"

He wrapped up mother and child and wheeled them outside. It was dawn.

Outside, I saw a row of small sparrows lined up and huddling together on the power line, as the ambulance door opened and the techs gently lifted Tammy and her new son inside.

One of them noticed something and exclaimed, "Will ya looka that! Ain't never seen one a them 'roun' heah."

Across the highway, sitting on the top branch of a large pine tree, was a golden eagle.

As the other tech was about to close the back door of the ambulance, Tammy called out, "We're going to name him David!"

The ambulance drove off, heading east into the sunrise. The little sparrows followed it.

The eagle took off from the pine tree, circled above my head, and flew in the opposite direction.

I waved at it.

That day, an eagle flew west.

In the aviation world, pilots honor the passing of their friends with the valedictory, "An eagle flew west."

Blue skies, forever, Country Boy.

R.A. Comunale is a semi-retired physician in family practice and a specialist in aviation medicine who lives and works out of his home office in Northern Virginia. He enjoys writing, gardening, electronics, pounding on a piano, and yelling at his dimwitted cat. He describes himself as an eccentric and iconoclast.

The cat is seeking palimony.